DESIRE

DOMS OF CLUB EDEN

LK SHAW

Desire, Doms of Club Eden Book 2
© 2016 by LK Shaw
Cover design © 2019 by Laura Hidalgo
All Rights Reserved.

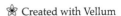 Created with Vellum

Want a FREE short story? Be sure to sign up for my newsletter and download your copy of A Birthday Spanking, a Doms of Club Eden prequel! http:// bit.ly/LKShawNewsletter

Doms of Club Eden

Submission

Desire

Redemption

Protect

Betrayal

My Christmas Dom

Absolution

Love Undercover Series

In Too Deep

Striking Distance

Atonement (Coming 2020)

Other Books

Love Notes: A Dark Romance

SEALs in Love

Say Yes

Black Light: Possession

Saving Evie: A Brotherhood Protectors

PROLOGUE

"Push."

I had never experienced such pain in all my sixteen years. Not even when my mother died. Pain in my body, but even more so, pain in my heart. I knew once I finished pushing, regret would fill every corner of my heart. Regret about my choices. Regret about the life I was giving up. Regret that I couldn't give this baby everything it deserved. Deep down, I knew this was the best decision I could make, even if it broke me in the process. I was sixteen years old. What kind of life could I provide a baby? I was still a child myself.

Another contraction hit, and a scream ripped through me as I bore down, pushing with all my might. No sooner did the echo of my scream fade than the cry of a baby filled the room. I sank into the bed, exhausted in body and spirit.

"It's a boy," came the voice from somewhere in the room. I heard the hustle of activity as the nurses prepared my baby — no, not *my* baby, *their* baby — to be handed over to his adoptive parents. I tried to ignore the crushing agony threatening to overwhelm me. Now was not the time. I could grieve later.

"Would you like to see him?" the nurse asked me, even as I started to shake my head. No, I didn't want to see him. I didn't want to look at his beautiful face or count his little fingers and toes. It wouldn't change a thing. It would do nothing but make my decision more difficult. I turned my head toward the wall and wished everything would just be over. I heard the nurse sigh softly in disappointment as she moved away. Before I knew it, the buzz of activity stopped and the quiet *snick* of the door closing sounded. I turned toward a soft caress against my cheek and immediately burst into heart-wrenching sobs as my father gently climbed into the hospital bed with me. He wrapped me in his comforting arms while we cried together as my heart shattered.

CHAPTER 1

"I need your help."

My whole body froze at the sound of the voice that haunted my dreams. Slowly, I raised my eyes from the papers scattered across my desk, schooling my features when I saw the stunning redhead standing at my office door. She fidgeted nervously in the doorway looking more beautiful than any woman had a right to. She was tall and all legs with enough curves to draw a man's attention. Long red locks cascaded down her back to dust the top of her ass. Blunt bangs framed her heart-shaped face, and her long lashes made her chocolate brown eyes appear large in her face, but not big enough to disguise the dark circles under them.

She also possessed an energy about her that instantly put me on high alert. I never expected to see Bridget Carter fidget. She always exhibited a self-assuredness that made me envious. I'd never seen her less than confident and bold as brass. Until today. Today, the boldness she typically displayed was missing. Nervousness, and perhaps even a little fear, had taken its place. As the owner of one of the top security and protection firms in the city, this was an expression I saw far too often.

"Bridget, please, come in and have a seat," I directed her as I rose from my chair. She closed the door behind her and made her way to the chair in front of my desk. I walked around the opposite side of my desk and propped my butt on it. She sat on the edge of her chair as if poised to flee quickly. It made me want to slay whatever demons were haunting her. And she definitely appeared haunted. "Now, tell me what you need my help with."

Her breasts distracted me briefly when she inhaled deeply, causing them to rise toward me. I shook myself mentally and brought my focus back to where it needed to be. After a minute, she continued to remain silent. I resisted the urge to reach out to comfort her. Being able to touch her was not something I was ready for, because I knew one touch wouldn't be enough. I typically used a soft, gentle voice when my cases brought me in contact with scared women and kids, but somehow, I knew I needed a different approach. I had observed Bridget often, and closely enough, at the BDSM club we both frequented, I knew how best to get her to respond. In my most firm Dom voice, I tried again. "Tell me what you need, Bridget. Now."

She startled, seeming to forget I stood less than three feet from her. However, my command broke through her thoughts, because she began to speak although still not making eye contact.

"I have a son," she said in a hushed voice, causing my mouth to fall open. Nothing Bridget said could have shocked me more. "Well, biologically, he's my son," she continued. "I gave him up for adoption years ago. I was only a kid myself, and I wanted him to have a better life than I would have been able to give him. I asked for an open adoption because, even though I couldn't take care of him, I still wanted to know he was okay. They sent me regular letters and pictures, but I never initiated contact, and I rebuffed every attempt his adoptive parents made for any type of visitation."

She fidgeted again, shifting slightly in the chair. Her voice quavered as she spoke. "Please don't judge me. Seeing him in person and hearing him call another woman 'mom' would have pushed me over the edge. The decision to give him up almost killed me. But it was a decision I had to make, even knowing I'd only be a part of his life peripherally."

She paused, as if gathering her thoughts, before she continued. "I left the option open that he be allowed access to my information when he turned eighteen. He's only thirteen, so I assumed if he had any interest in contacting me, it wouldn't be for another five years. Except two days ago, I received a phone call. It only lasted a few seconds, and I don't even know if it was really him. I only heard, 'I think you're my mother. Please, help me,' and then a scuffle in the background before the line went dead."

Bridget stopped speaking and finally raised her eyes to meet mine. What I saw in them gutted me. Unable to resist touching her any longer, I moved from my perch and knelt at her feet. I laid one hand on top of hers, which she had been wringing in her lap. Then, I reached up with my other hand to wipe away the lone tear that traced a path down her cheek. "I need you to tell me everything."

7

I told my assistant to hold all my calls, and for the next hour, Bridget explained to me that, right before she'd turned sixteen she discovered she was pregnant. Her mom died when Bridget was young, so her father raised her. He worked two jobs to support them, and when she became pregnant she knew there was only one option. She located an adoption agency and found the perfect adoptive family. Immediately after the birth of the baby, Bridget turned him over to them without even seeing him, because she thought it would be easier not to become attached. The adoptive parents made multiple attempts throughout the years to initiate contact, but Bridget never felt ready. The only information she was able to provide were their names and the return address used on the mail she'd received from them. "Connor, what if it was Alex? Why would he be calling me and not his parents? Especially asking for help. He sounded scared. Please, can you help me? I don't know where else to turn."

I instinctively knew helping Bridget would test me like nothing before. Not only because I might be a little in love with her, but because something deep inside told me this case would bring forth demons I'd fought hard to bury. But this wasn't about me. It was about Bridget, and God knew I would move heaven and Earth to find and destroy anything that threatened her or anyone she cared about.

ONCE BRIDGET LEFT, I sat in my office contemplating everything she'd told me. I started my own security and protection firm, Blacklight Securities, eight years ago after busting my ass to rise above all the bad shit in my past. I wanted to be in a position where I could help people who didn't know where to turn. People like my mother. When I opened my doors for business, there were no employees beyond me. After the first year, the company had grown enough for me to hire a couple of associates. By the third year, over twenty men and women were in my employ. I continued to keep my employee list small, but on occasion, I hired an independent contractor for special cases.

I'm a member of an exclusive BDSM club called Club Eden where I met fellow Dominant, Donovan Jeffries. Donovan is a lawyer, and former military. He put me in contact with some of his sources in the government, and I lucked out in getting several high paying government contracts. Most of our cases involve protecting a visiting dignitary or his family, but on occasion, we're hired for personal protection by wealthy businessmen.

My company is also known for taking on cases most other security companies have passed on. Mostly because they thought they were too dignified to be hired for what essentially amounted to high paying babysitting gigs. These jobs certainly weren't ideal, but beggars couldn't be choosers. Now though, we are able to pick and choose our own cases. I also do occasional pro bono work for one of the local battered women's shelters. If only my mother could see me now.

Luckily, I'm currently in between cases. Not that it would have mattered. I would have dropped everything the second the words asking for help crossed Bridget's lips. From here on out my main focus would be on Bridget and her son. *Her son!* I was still in shock by this bombshell she'd dropped. That she had a child was the last thing I would have thought she would tell me. I wasn't sure how I felt about it yet, but it didn't matter. I would have dropped everything the second the words asking for help crossed Bridget's lips. The first thing I needed to find out was who'd made that phone call. And if it was Alex, where were his parents? And why did he sound desperate for help?

CHAPTER 2

SITTING in my car outside Connor's building, I tried to calm my racing heart. A gamut of emotions raced through me now that I knew someone would help me. Scratch that. Now that I knew Connor would help me. First and foremost was relief, followed by continued worry for Alex. I didn't realize how desperate and frenzied I'd become to find out if the caller was Alex. It was killing me not knowing if he was safe and sound.

But the most surprising emotion? Lust. Although it shouldn't have come as a surprise. I'd always had an unhealthy fascination with Connor Black. We were both members of Eden, so I saw him frequently. We'd never scened together though. In fact, I had never seen him scene with any of the subs. There had only been a handful of times I watched as he took a sub into a private room. I would never admit to anyone, myself included, how often I wondered what it would be like if I were the one walking through one of those doors with him.

I gathered my courage one night and asked Gina what

the experience was like since I knew she was one of the few subs he'd played with privately. She was also one of my employees at the upscale boutique I managed, so I trusted her completely and knew she wouldn't ask any probing questions. She was evasive, only saying Connor was a generous Dom. Whatever the hell that meant. But, it had piqued my curiosity more than I would admit. Enough that I was constantly on the lookout for who he took to the back rooms. Which, oddly, only happened to be a sub here or there. It only made me wonder why he didn't scene publicly.

Connor wasn't handsome in the typical sense, his face was too craggy and rough for that, but he was built like a brick house with wide, muscular shoulders that tapered to a narrow waist. His biceps were so large, I knew my fingers wouldn't touch if I wrapped my hands around them. His close cut, dark brown hair didn't have a fleck of gray although I thought he had to be at least five years older than me.

As much as I was fascinated by Connor, I was in no way looking for a relationship. I made that clear to all the Doms I scened with. I enjoyed my single life as a thirty-year-old woman with no responsibilities. Did I, on occasion, wonder what it would be like to have a Dom of my own? Yes, but not enough that I wanted to throw my single status away. Besides, my heart was no longer available. It had shattered beyond repair the day I gave up my baby. I didn't feel it was fair to a man, knowing that I could never love him. I didn't have it in me to love. It hurt too much. So, I stuck with either dating until the guy finally realized I was serious about my stance on relationships and broke it off with me or playing with the Doms who approached me at Eden.

Now that the burden of Alex had been partially lifted

from my shoulders, I left Blacklight Securities and headed to work. The store I managed was a popular, upscale clothing boutique in the heart of downtown. I'd put myself through fashion design school even though my dad wanted to help. But I needed to do something for myself, so I had gone to school full-time and worked two part-time jobs at two different boutiques to support myself.

I lived at home until I was twenty-five and had finally been promoted to full-time store manager at one of the boutiques. By then I'd also saved enough money to put a down payment on a small, two-bedroom condo. The city had renovated an old warehouse building in an up-and-coming area of downtown and converted it into condos.

Normally, I would have walked to work since I lived less than two miles away from the boutique, but since I needed to see Connor first, I had pulled my beat-up clunker out of the garage. Which meant finding parking was going to be a bitch. After circling the block three or four times, I finally spied an open spot. I pulled in and walked the two blocks to work. If it wasn't going to make me later than I already was, I would have just taken the car back home and walked.

The overhead bell jingled as I rushed through the door. Gina peeked her head around a display mannequin she was dressing and smiled at me in welcome. I was always grateful she never talked about the night I asked her about Connor.

"Hey, boss lady. You're late," she teased.

I put on my best smile as I moved through the store. "The benefits of being top bitch," I joked. "How are things going this morning? Did the latest shipment arrive?"

She snorted at my "top bitch" comment. "This place is the only time you're ever a top anything, and you know it. And the delivery truck left about ten minutes ago. All the boxes are stacked in the back room waiting for you to check off the inventory. I know how particular you are about it."

"Thanks, G. I'm going to head back there now to get started. Holler if you need any help out here."

I made my way to the back room where I started unpacking the boxes and checking off my list of items to make sure that all the pieces were there. I'd found some gorgeous retro dresses at this online consignment shop I purchased from on occasion, so I snatched them up. I also had one of my buyers hit an estate sale to buy and ship me everything she thought I could sell. I had been rifling through the inventory for about an hour when I heard Gina yell out that I had a phone call.

I walked over to the desk and pressed the flashing button to answer the call on hold.

"Hello, this is Bridget."

Silence.

"Hello, may I help you?" I asked. I waited another few seconds, and as I moved to hang up, a small voice whispered, causing the tiny hairs on the back of my neck to stand at attention.

"Hello, can you hear me?"

In a frenzy, I rattled off questions. "Oh my God, Alex, is that you? Are you okay? Where are your parents? What's going on?"

The young boy continued speaking in a hushed whisper. "I can't talk long, he'll be back any second. My parents are dead. I need your help, please. I don't know where else to turn."

I gasped at the news his parents were dead. "Alex, tell me where —"

"I'm sorry, I have to go. He's coming." *Click.*

"No, wait. Alex? Alex?" I yelled into the phone, but it was too late. The line was already dead. I screeched in frustration and fear. That was twice now that he'd called, and I had gotten no information. I didn't even know where he was or why he needed help. This was all my fault. I hung up the phone, my hands shaking. I didn't even realize I was crying until a tear splashed on my hand.

"Boss, you okay back there? I thought I heard you yell." Gina poked her head through the doorway. Not wanting her to see how shaken up I was, I kept my back to the door as I assured her everything was fine.

Surprised by how calm I sounded, I added, "Thanks for checking on me, Gina. I didn't mean to startle you. I'll be out in a minute."

She hesitated before she replied with a quiet "okay" and turned around to walk back out to the front of the store. I gathered my composure, pasted on a fake smile, and headed out to the front to face the rest of my day, all the while, dying inside not knowing what was happening to Alex.

CHAPTER 3

I SPENT four days looking into the adoption of Bridget's son and finding out what I could about the boy and his parents. In my search, I discovered Christopher and Gail Shipman had been killed in a car accident two months prior. Because the Shipmans had foolishly not drawn up a Will, the courts were responsible for the boy. Even though Alex was biologically Bridget's son, she had given up her parental rights, so she wasn't a candidate to home Alex. In fact, she obviously hadn't even been notified of their deaths. Mrs. Shipman, whose parents were also dead, had been an only child, and the only closest living relative willing to take responsibility for Alex was his uncle, his adoptive father's older brother.

Malcolm Shipman was single, forty-eight years old, and lived in a small neighborhood in the suburbs. He had no criminal record, not even a parking ticket, and was steadily employed at a big name appliance store. It only took me a single day to find out where Alex was living, so I followed Malcolm for the next three days to observe some of his habits. As soon as Alex left the house and started walking the three blocks to the bus stop, Malcolm would head to the gym where he worked out for precisely an hour. After that, he went to work where he appeared jovial and friendly with all the customers who came into the store. After his shift was over, Malcolm headed straight home and was never home later than 5:30 pm, as if he commanded everyone out of his way. Every night, all the lights went off in the house at exactly 10:00. His routine seemed almost military in its pattern, with no variation..

Alex was a little trickier to observe since he was in school all day. The one thing I did notice during Alex's trek to and from the bus stop was he didn't seem to have any friends. He got on and off the school bus alone, and no one walked with him the three blocks from the bus stop to the house. Which seemed unusual for a boy his age, even one who had recently moved to a new neighborhood. He also appeared sullen and unhappy. Granted, he was a thirteen-, almost fourteen-year-old boy whose parents had recently died, but another expression lurked behind his eyes. An expression I tried to ignore, because it reminded me too much of "him". I avoided thinking of "him" whenever possible, because he made me feel weak and ashamed. Unfortunately, he snuck into my thoughts when I least expected and more often than I wished. I pushed back the memories and brought my attention back to Alex.

The thing that struck me the most was Alex's resemblance to Bridget. I had become almost an expert in all things Bridget, and I noticed it immediately. Alex had a slight auburn tint to his hair, and he possessed the same large, chocolate-brown eyes surrounded by long, lush eyelashes that grown women would kill for. If not for the more masculine features I could detect, like a strong, square jawline, he could have been described as almost too pretty.

Bridget was worried to death about Alex, so I knew I needed to at least let her know that he'd been located. I also needed to figure out a way to approach Alex without Malcolm being aware, which looked like it was going to be a challenge since, so far, he hadn't spent a lot of time out of his presence. However, since becoming an adult, I've never been one to back away from a challenge.

Even from a distance, I sensed an edge to Alex. An edge no thirteen-year-old boy should have. Something felt wrong about the whole situation, and Alex had obviously called Bridget for a reason.

I figured my best bet would be to try and catch him close to the bus stop on his way to school. It was in the opposite direction of the gym Malcolm went to, and I had yet to spot him coming this way. If that didn't work out, then I would try during the twenty minutes or so between the time Alex got home from school and Malcolm arrived home from work, but I needed to do a few more days of recon to make sure. I wouldn't take any chances with Alex's safety.

It was close to 4:00 pm, and I sat in my office debating what I was going to say to Bridget about Alex. I wanted her to know I'd located him, but I also didn't want her trying to make contact until I knew exactly what I was dealing with. I took a deep, bracing breath and reached for the phone to try and reach her before she left her office for the day.

"Unique Boutique, this is Bridget, how may I help you?" God, her voice alone made me hard.

"It's Connor," I said, succinctly.

"Oh my God, Connor, I've been waiting for you to call

me for days. Have you found Alex? Is he okay?" She was almost hysterical.

"Yes, I found Alex, and he seems to be safe at the moment," I told her calmly. "I haven't —"

"Where is he? I need to see him."

"Bridget," I chided gently, "I'm trying to explain if you would please just listen. Now, as I was saying, Alex seems to be safe. I haven't had a chance to speak to him, but I hope to have the opportunity in the next couple of days. There is nothing you can do right now other than wait for me to talk to him. I need to find out if he was the one who called you and why he thinks he needs help. You came to me. Let me do my job."

"I know it was him, Connor," she started, an edge of panic in her voice. "He called again the day I left your office. He said his parents were dead. He sounded scared and said he couldn't talk long, because 'he' would be back soon. Who is 'he'? What's going on, Connor? Alex is my son, and I deserve to know, damn it."

"Why the fuck didn't you tell me he called again, Bridget?" I snapped in irritation. I needed all the information I could get, and her withholding this from me, intentionally or not, pissed me off. I knew I sounded harsh, but I couldn't seem to control my emotions knowing a child might be in danger. I waited impatiently for her response.

I heard a slight sniff in the background and knew she was crying. "I'm sorry, Connor. I just didn't think. It took me by surprise, and I've been sitting by the phone waiting for him to call again. I swear if he calls again, I'll let you know immediately."

I sighed. "I understand, Bridget, but you need to keep me in the loop. That's why you came to me. I'm going to try and talk to Alex one day on his way to school. But I need to be careful, just in case. I don't want to do anything that might endanger him, especially after what you just told me about his last phone call. I'll let you know when I have news. As hard as it's going to be, I need you to be patient. Can you do that?"

Silence reigned, and I could feel her hesitation on the other end of the line. As much as I was avoiding it, I knew there was only going to be one way for me to handle Bridget. As with any scene, I had to take control. Otherwise, things were going to go to shit.

"Bridget," I admonished. "You *will* be patient, do you understand me?"

As though on autopilot, she replied immediately, "Yes, Sir, I understand."

"Good girl," I praised. "I'll call you in a couple days. Until then, try not to worry."

I hung up the phone and sighed. God, this case was going to be the death of me. I was already feeling the anxiety and tension start to creep in, my mind was preparing for battle. And my gut told me that was only the beginning.

CHAPTER 4

It was Saturday morning, and five days had passed since I first started watching Alex and Malcolm Shipman. I sat in my car down the street from Malcolm's house doing surveillance when I caught a break. I watched as Malcolm's black Tesla Model S 70D backed out of the driveway and started down the street. From the moment I first saw the car, I wondered how someone who worked at an appliance store could afford a car like this, but I pushed it out of my mind. As the car passed me, I noticed he was alone and knew this was my chance. Because I didn't know where he was going or how long he'd be gone, I waited ten minutes to make sure he wasn't going to come back for something he might have forgotten. I jumped out of my car, jogged over to the house, and glanced around, taking in my surroundings, before knocking on the front door. I waited to see if Alex would answer and began to wonder if my luck had run out when the door slowly opened a crack.

I stared into questioning brown eyes. "Hi."

"What do you want?" came the tentative question. I

noticed that Alex remained alert and kept his hands on the door, as if knowing he might need to quickly slam it closed. I also noticed something up close that I hadn't noticed before. He was skinny. Not slim, like a tall boy whose body hadn't quite caught up with its height yet, but skinny. Like a growing boy who wasn't eating as much as he should.

"Are you Alex?" I asked softly, trying to project a tone that proclaimed I didn't pose a threat. My size intimidated most people, so I tried to make myself appear affable, especially to the women and children I encountered in my line of work.

Questioning eyes suddenly turned terrified. He straightened his spine despite the fear pouring out of him. With a contradicting boldness and a lift of his chin that was all Bridget, he answered, "Who wants to know?"

"My name is Connor. I'm friends with your mom."

He frowned at my answer. "I think you have the wrong person. My mother is dead."

I cleared my throat. "I meant your birth mother, Bridget Carter. I understand you called her a few days ago. She's worried sick about you and asked me to make sure you were okay. Were you the one who called her?"

With my words, a new emotion flashed across his face. An emotion that I had no trouble deciphering. Relief. His muscles relaxed, and the tension left his shoulders and legs as I watched him almost collapse against the door. In an instant though, his expression changed. He glanced around warily as if nervous to be seen talking to me.

"You can't be here when he comes back. I'll get in trouble. You need to go." Alex tried to close the door, which I stopped with the flat of my hand.

"What do you mean, you'll 'get in trouble'? Alex, are you

in danger? Tell me. It's the only way I can help you. You can trust me." I encouraged him to talk to me.

"I'm sorry to have bothered her. Please, tell her I'm okay. She doesn't need to worry about me. It was a mistake to call." I knew where he got his stubbornness from.

I also knew he wasn't going to say any more. I kept my one hand on the door and dug into my pocket with the other. I removed my hand from the door, but stuck my foot out to brace against the base of the door while I opened my wallet and pulled out my card. I held it out to him.

"Take this. It's my card with my contact info, including my personal cell phone number. If you need something, *anything*, call me. Anytime, day or night. Whatever is going on, Alex, you're not alone. Like I said before, you can trust me." I waited patiently to see if he'd accept the offering.

He snatched the card out of my hand and, with a burst of strength, slammed the door shut, catching me off balance enough that I almost fell backward. I sighed in frustration and took off back to my car, hoping that Alex would take my words to heart.

I drove to the gym to work out my frustrations. And to release the inner demons that threatened to overwhelm me after my short talk with Alex. Everything about Alex screamed at me. He put me in mind of that other boy. The one I constantly tried to banish, but who never ceased to show up when I least expected it. Thoughts of him brought up feelings of weakness, insecurity, vulnerability, and worse, shame. Feelings I was uncomfortable with and fought hard to suppress.

I worked out hard, pushing myself past the point of pain and exhaustion, attempting to banish the weakness that, if I let it, would consume me. With sweat pouring down my face and body, I headed to the shower room. I stood in the private shower stall, hand braced on the wall in front of me, head bowed as the scalding hot water sluiced down my body. Without conscious thought, Bridget's face flashed through my head, causing a groan to escape my lips and my cock to harden. *Fuck.*

I tortured myself with thoughts of her. She was too good for someone like me, half a man. Someone who couldn't give her the things she needed. Someone who wanted things she couldn't handle. My body warred with my brain. I knew that nothing was ever going to happen between us, but my body hadn't caught up with my brain yet. My body didn't care, it only wanted. I pictured her long legs wrapped around my back as I roughly pounded my cock into her. Her nails scored my back causing blood to rise to the surface as she marked me.

With thoughts of thrusting in and out of her hot pussy running through my head, I moved my free hand down my body to grasp the base of my cock, and I began lightly stroking myself at first. I continued stroking, matching the rhythm of my imaginary scene with Bridget. I pummeled her cunt as my strokes became faster and my grip tightened almost painfully. Up and down I moved my hand and my balls drew up in anticipation. With a final stroke, my cock erupted in an explosion that left me fighting for breath. When the tremors faded, I sagged against the wall of the shower.

After I recovered from my release, I finished washing up and exited the shower. I stood in the empty locker room and stared at my reflection in the mirror. Scars dotted my chest. But those were nothing compared to the scars that graced my back. I tried to picture my body from a woman's viewpoint. The one and only time I fucked a woman while I was naked, she drew back in disgust at my disfigurement. She tried to hide it, but it was too late. I saw the look she gave me, and it was a look I never forgot and one I ever wanted to see again. After that, I limited my sexual encounters. During the few I did have, I made sure my upper body was covered at all times. Having a woman turn from me in disgust was not an experience I was anxious to repeat.

I tried to satisfy by dominant side with activities that didn't include intercourse. I was never fully satisfied though. I always held back a part of myself when I played. A part I kept hidden. Mostly out of fear of what I would do if I released it, but partially out of shame.

I quickly dressed, and even though I'd just had a powerful orgasm, it wasn't enough. I needed more. After so many years of being at someone else's mercy, I needed to be in control. I needed the rush of power that came from dominating someone. It appeared a visit to Eden was on the schedule for the night. I ignored the thought that maybe I'd see Bridget. I knew she bounced from one Dom to another by choice. She didn't want more than a casual relationship. I knew what I wanted, even if I couldn't have it. Which meant I needed to guard my heart. I didn't need to add a broken heart to all the other fucked up things that were wrong with me.

CHAPTER 5

EDEN. My home away from home. I loved coming here. It was my release after a long week. And this week had been especially taxing. I took in the sights and sounds around me. The purplish glow of the dimmed lights and the moans of satisfied couples echoing in the air comforted me. I glanced around trying to catch a glimpse of my friend, Penny, who had recently married her Dom, Marcus. Instead of her, though, my gaze honed in on Connor leaning against the bar, staring out into the crowd with an indecipherable expression on his face.

During all the times I discreetly watched him in the past, one thing I noticed was that he never talked much. He was more a silent observer, and more than once, I felt his stare boring into me, but whenever I turned to catch his gaze, he always looked away. His actions only made me want to know more about this enigmatic Dom.

Without conscious thought, I made my way over to him. He turned his head when I stepped into his personal space.

"Good evening, Sir," I purred, causing him to raise a

single eyebrow in surprise. I tried to hide my own shock at my flirty tone. Never before had I openly flirted with Connor, and I had definitely never referred to him as *Sir* in a suggestive way. I had a hard time remembering us ever having a private, one-on-one conversation inside the club. In fact, I couldn't think of a single one. He never approached me to scene, and we didn't hang out in the same social circle outside of the club. He didn't even attend any of the munches. The only real friends we shared were Penny and Marcus, and I spoke to Connor only in passing during their wedding celebration since we had both been in the bridal party. Our longest conversation had taken place in his office at the beginning of the week when I approached him about Alex.

"Bridget," he responded with a wary nod, confused by my approach. *You're not the only one confused, buddy.* I smiled at him and leaned closer, ignoring the warning bells going off inside my head that told me I was biting off more than I could chew. I wasn't a warning bells kind of woman. I was confident in my sexuality, and I never shied away from what I wanted. And tonight, for some unknown reason, I wanted Connor.

"See anything you like?" I asked, pushing my half exposed tits out for his inspection. His gaze dropped to my chest, and his nostrils flared before he raised his glance back up to my face.

Connor hesitated briefly before speaking. "I think you're playing with fire, sub."

I shrugged in nonchalance. "Maybe I want to get burned."

"You should be careful what you wish for, Bridget. You may not be able to handle what I give you," he warned.

I laughed lightly at his warning. "That sounds like a dare, Sir. And I've never been one to pass on a dare. Life's too short to play things safe."

I held my breath as I waited to see if Connor would take the bait. The ball was now in his court. I wanted to see if he'd continue our game. I could tell he was battling with himself, indecision crossing his face. I couldn't help wondering what was holding him back. I was blatantly flirting with him and practically handing myself to him on a silver platter. He stared at me for so long I actually started to become uncomfortable. And I was never uncomfortable in Eden. I began to think he was going to dismiss me, when he suddenly moved away from the bar and grabbed my hand. My pulse fluttered when, without another word spoken, he led me toward the private rooms at the back of the common area of the club. This wasn't my first trip back here, but this time, I knew it would be different. More. I wasn't sure how I felt about that either, but I ignored the feeling.

In the years he'd been a member of Eden, I noticed side glances from Connor that I always had difficulty interpreting. I intentionally avoided trying to decipher them because I didn't want to know what they meant. I could admit to a fascination with Connor Black, but it ended there. While it might seem a bit arrogant to think I held that kind of power, I had no desire to be the reason behind someone's broken heart.

We reached the second room on the right, and with a hard knock to ensure it was empty, Connor opened the door and made room for me to precede him into it. I looked around at a room I had seen many times before, but for some reason, it looked different tonight. I heard the *snick* of the door closing behind me, and my heartbeat accelerated with

31

the knowledge that, after all these years, my curiosity about Connor Black would finally be satisfied. Once this night was over, I could move on to another Dom, and my fascination with Connor would be done.

"Strip and stay facing forward."

I started to turn my head, but the hard slap to my ass and the repeated "face forward" in that deep voice left me with no choice but to obey the command. I slowly began to unlace my corset as I listened for any echoed movement behind me that signified Connor was undressing as well. The only thing I heard was the sound of my own breathing. I removed every article of clothing until I stood completely nude. Then I waited. After what felt like an eternity, my hair was pushed over my shoulder and a soft caress tickled down the length of my spine, from my neck to the crack of my ass. A shiver washed over me at the contact, and wetness glistened on my inner thighs. No one had turned me on this quickly with only the barest of touches. It made me nervous to know that Connor was the one to do it.

Connor ran his fingers across my shoulders and down my arms, the hairs on my arms rising from the arousal that coursed through my body. I thought the whisper of a kiss ghosted across my skin in the dip where my neck and shoulder met, but it happened so fast and was so light it was hard to tell. I kept waiting for him to say something. What, I don't know. But the continued silence was slightly unnerving. This was the first time I hadn't negotiated a scene ahead of time. I always had the "I'm only here to have fun" and "I'm not looking for a D/s relationship" discussion before I played with anyone. Connor was right when he said I was playing with fire.

Finally, he spoke. "Get on the bed on your hands and knees. Don't turn around."

I followed his command as my feet drew me closer to the bed. I crawled up to the head of it and positioned myself as he'd instructed, my ass and pussy on full display. I wondered at his refusal to let me see him though. Ignoring the thought for now, I arched my back and opened my legs a little wider pushing my girly bits closer into his view. It never hurt to show a man exactly what he was getting.

The bed dipped behind me with the weight of Connor joining me. My pussy was wet with need, and I gasped as rough-skinned hands gripped my hips tightly and calloused thumbs rubbed along the back of my thighs, just under the crease of my ass cheeks. His touch ignited a spark and an electric shock flowed through me. It was a zing I had never felt before with any other Dom, and it left me slightly unnerved. A moan of arousal sounded in the otherwise quiet room, and I realized it came from me.

"I need more, Sir." My body twitched in anticipation, and I pushed back against his hands.

"You'll get what I give you, Bridget. Nothing more, nothing less. Now, stop trying to top from the bottom."

I groaned at his words. I wanted his mouth, his cock. All of it.

I endured several minutes of his hands running along my body, from the soles of my feet, up my calves, and over the roundness of my ass as he bypassed where I most wanted him. He stroked along my sides as he leaned into me with his clothed body. The texture of his pants abraded my sensitive skin. His erection pressed into the crack of my ass. He moved away from me, his hands skimming along my back, before I could press against him.

Without warning, the crack of his palm slapping against my right ass cheek reverberated around the room.

"Oh, God," I bit out, followed by a satisfied moan. Rough hands grasped my hips again, and a gentle kiss and swipe of his tongue eased the sting. I felt the slight pressure of Connor's teeth as he nipped at my other cheek. The contradictory sensations caused more wetness to drip down my already coated thighs.

Hot, humid breath danced across my pussy, and before I could blink, Connor ran his tongue up my slit before dipping inside my pussy to lap up the cream flowing from it. He plunged his tongue further into my cunt and drank from me as I squirmed in excitement and ecstasy, helpless against the assault, my body balanced on the edge of a cliff, ready to fly. This man's touch did things to me that no man's had ever done before. I didn't want to think about what that meant.

"Yes," I breathed out.

His tongue shifted and began circling the rim of my asshole at the same time he thrust two fingers deep inside me. The pressure of his fingers hitting that elusive spot most men had trouble finding sent a tidal wave of feeling rushing through me, and I screamed out my pleasure as my climax hit. My arms gave out, and I dropped to my forearms as my forehead pressed into the mattress below me while I tried to catch my breath.

Connor pressed his cock against me again as his hands reached under my armpits to pull me upright so my back was now flush to his front. I briefly frowned when I noted he was still fully clothed. I wanted to feel his skin against mine, but the thought was chased away when he cupped my breasts in his large hands and pinched my nipples hard. The pleasure-pain radiated straight to my core still spasming from the orgasm that had ripped through my body only moments before, and I still hadn't caught my breath.

The echo of Connor's heavy breathing rasped against my ear as he groaned. "God, you feel so good. I want to take you hard and rough and shove my cock so far up your pussy you won't be able to tell where you end and I begin. You can't even imagine all the fucked up things I want to do to you. You'd run scared if you knew." He pulled my nipples forward, pinching them hard at the same time he stretched them until I inhaled sharply at the pain. He continued to pinch and pull, and when I didn't think I could take anymore, he released them.

"I want to put clamps on your nipples and watch them pebble as I tighten the screw. Then I want to hear you scream as the blood comes rushing back in when I remove them." He moved one hand from my breast and cupped my mound as he continued speaking. "I want to see you fuck yourself with a dildo as your ass rides my cock. Then I want to see your tears as I redden your ass with a crop."

Holy shit. His words sent a trickle of unease running through me. He was right. The things he wanted to do to me did scare me a little. I wasn't scared of the pain or his intense, graphic descriptions. Okay, so maybe I was a little scared of the pain. What had me the most scared was the fact that my body suddenly began craving those things. "You don't scare me, you know," I assured him. "You may think you do, but you don't."

He laughed softly against my hair. "Oh Bridget, you sweet, naive girl. I scare myself." He lightly kissed my cheek before pulling away. Cold air danced across my back, and I missed the heat of him surrounding me. The mattress shifted when he moved off it. I quickly turned around, dropping to my butt and watched, open-mouthed, as he gathered my clothes off the floor. He handed them to me while I sat in shock that he appeared to be leaving.

"That's it?" I questioned. "You're leaving me? I mean...you're leaving?"

"You got what you wanted," he answered with an expression I couldn't make out behind his hooded eyes.

I snorted, and a sound that could only be described as a laugh escaped. "You have no idea what I want, Connor. You never asked me. How do you know I don't want or need the same things you do? Isn't that the purpose of contracts and negotiations? We discuss hard and soft limits." Anger built inside me, and it threatened to burst as I continued. "Tonight was the first time you've ever touched me. You didn't ask me what my limits are. There was no communication. I take partial blame for that. My need for you overpowered my common sense and rational thinking. I should have paused things so we could talk about the scene, but I didn't. And now look where we are. Both of us angry and mutually unsatisfied."

An eyebrow quirked as he replied, "I'm pretty sure you were satisfied."

With his words, I jumped off the bed and began dressing. "Fuck you, Connor. I would hardly call an orgasm that anyone could have given me 'satisfied'. I was *pleasured*, but that is the extent of it. *Satisfied* means we would both be naked in this bed after you fucked my brains out. *That* would have *satisfied* me. Now, I'm just *pissed off*."

It was his turn to stare at me in open-mouthed shock. My movements were jerky as I continued throwing my clothes on. Connor watched in silence as I stomped over and snatched my shoes up off the floor. I reached down with one shoe in my hand and slammed my foot into it. First one, then the other. Needing the last word, I threw out, "For your information, I've always been utterly fascinated with you. I have never wanted more than an occasional scene with a Dom. Until tonight. You gave me a taste of what could have been between us. For a second I wanted…I don't know what I wanted, but a quick fuck wasn't it."

I made my way to the door, fists clenched in an effort not to flip him off. I jerked it open and spun around so I could see his face as I spoke. "You seem to know what you want, but you're too scared to take it. I need a Dom who not only knows what he wants, but has the balls to go after it. That man is obviously not you. I appreciate everything you've done so far in helping me find Alex, but I think it would be best if we parted ways here. I'll find someone else to help me. Thanks anyway, Connor." With my final words, I walked out the door, closing it quietly behind me.

CHAPTER 6

FUCK. What was I thinking the other night? I completely fucked things up, and I don't know how to fix them. I don't know what the hell I thought was going to happen when I took Bridget into that room. I stayed away from her at the club for a reason. Her flirtation shocked the shit out of me. But once she batted those fucking eyes at me, I was a goner. I was always the one in control. Until her. Then my control went straight out the window. All I know now was I never should have touched her. Because one touch will never be enough.

I was sure she couldn't handle the things I wanted to do to her. Although if I were honest with myself, I was the one who couldn't handle it. I kept my desires buried deep. I was afraid I would lose control once I unleashed the beast inside me. And then, I'd be just like him. But after the way she'd left, my chances of touching her again were nil, so it was a moot point.

It had been a day and a half since our night at Eden, and I spent the entire time replaying everything in my mind. I remembered the sounds of Bridget coming apart under my hand and how sweet she tasted. Like the ripest strawberries dipped in cream. I had jacked off more times in the last two days than I had in the last month. All because of the best sex I'd never had.

Even though she told me to back off and that she no longer needed or wanted my help, I had no intention of letting this case go. Someone was threatening Alex, even if he wouldn't admit it, and I needed to stop it. I had no other choice.

It was 6:00 a.m. on Monday, and I'd be damned if I was going to wait another day before speaking to Alex again. I quickly showered and dressed before heading to my car. I drove the forty minutes to Malcolm Shipman's side of town and parked within sight of the school bus stop.

At approximately 7:10, I saw Alex, head down and shuffling along, making his way along the sidewalk. Even though I had lost long since faith in any higher power, I said a little prayer under my breath that Malcolm had kept to his daily routine and was already at the gym. I exited my car and jogged over to start walking next to Alex. He startled in surprise when I matched him stride for stride, but didn't say a word.

"Have you given any more thought to my visit the other day?" I questioned him as we stood slightly away from the other kids loitering at the stop.

"I told you already, I made a mistake calling her," Alex ground out.

"Yeah, I know what you told me. Let's just say I don't quite believe you, kid. Who are you protecting?" I crossed my arms and stared intently at him. It felt wrong to try and intimidate him into giving up his secrets, but there wasn't a chance in hell I was going to walk away without some information.

About the same time I finished my question, the congregated kids all started shuffling to the curb as if sensing the impending arrival of the bus. Alex moved from his position to get in line. As he attempted to step past me, I reached out to stop him with a hand on his arm. He inhaled sharply with a pained hiss and winced, pulling away from my touch. *What the hell?*

"Stop right there, kid. What's wrong with your arm?"

"Nothing," he replied, too quickly.

"Alex." I drew out his name in slight warning.

"It's noth—nothing," he stuttered.

"God damn it, Alex, show me," I hissed, causing Alex to jump back in fear and the other kids to turn sharply to see what was going on.

I closed my eyes, inhaling deeply and blowing out my breath in a huff, trying to gather my patience. "I'm sorry. I didn't mean to yell at you. I'm not going to hurt you. Now, will you please show me your arm?"

Hesitantly, he raised his shirtsleeve past his elbow, and I caught a glimpse of the large purple bruise in the shape of a thumb around his bicep. I gently reached out so as to not startle him again, and I pushed the sleeve out of the way to see the bruises wrap around the rest of his arm, each one in the shape of a finger. Fury clouded my vision and immediately my brain flashed back to another place and time. To another frightened boy with similar bruises. Alex must have sensed the rage coursing through my veins, because he pulled out of my grasp and pushed his sleeve down to cover the marks, as if that would make them magically disappear.

"It was an accident," he explained.

"Bullshit," I scoffed. "You don't 'accidentally' get that kind of bruising, Alex. Who touched you?"

"My uncle." He rushed to continue, "But it wasn't on purpose. He was grilling out, and I was playing around near the grill even after he told me to stop, and I tripped. I would have fallen into it if he hadn't grabbed me. So, you see, it was an accident."

My gaze bore into his, trying to read the truth in his words. It sounded like a reasonable excuse, but in my line of work I was trained to filter lies from the truth. And everything coming out of his mouth sounded like a load of shit. I didn't understand why he was trying to protect his uncle. *Lies are often told to protect oneself,* came a voice in the back of my head. Didn't I know it. Some of the most destructive lies are the ones we tell ourselves. How often had I made excuses for what was happening to me?

I had to give him credit. He maintained direct eye contact with me for longer than I expected. But before long, he dropped his gaze and shuffled nervously as though he knew I saw right through him. Sadly, there was nothing I could do. I had an unfounded supposition that, without proof, didn't mean a damn thing. I needed to put a call into an acquaintance of mine on the police force.

As I was about to question Alex further, even knowing nothing more would come of the conversation, the school bus rolled to stop in front of the crowd. Alex continued his attempt to pass me and join the group beginning to board the waiting bus, and this time, I didn't stop him. He paused briefly and turned his head to peer back at me.

"Look, I appreciate your concern, but there is nothing you can do. Just let it go. Everything is fine. I'm sorry I dragged her into this. Please, just leave me alone." The

42

sadness, and underlying fear I recognized all too well, tore at my gut as all I could do was watch him disappear into the bowels of the bus. I remained standing there, staring after the bus as it rolled away from the curb, taking a scared boy with it. *Fuck.*

CHAPTER 7

TWO DAYS. That's how long it had been since I walked out of Eden following the cataclysmic scene with Connor. Pissed and hurt didn't even begin to describe my emotions. For that brief moment in time, Connor had made me question myself and my heart. Never before had I felt such a strong bond with a Dom who scened with me. Every scene before this one had been about giving up control and the gratification I received. I thought that was how I wanted it. Until him.

It wasn't always sexual gratification either. Often it was the cathartic release of emotions bottled up inside me. I was happy with how I lived my life. I was content with the peripheral emotional connection I received during aftercare. Except Connor made me want more. A deeper and more meaningful emotional connection. Not necessarily a relationship, because I wasn't ready for that, and I didn't know if I ever would be. But something other than a single scene with a random Dom. Then he had to go and fuck it up. And it pissed me off.

What hurt though was that he didn't try to understand

me or my needs. It also hurt that he didn't trust me with his needs; he assumed I'd run scared. That I wasn't strong enough for him. Even though he tried to hide it, I knew he'd judged me when I told him about Alex. He thought I was weak and selfish for giving him up. I knew this, because the expression in his eyes matched the one I saw every day when I looked at myself in the mirror. There was nothing in my life I regretted more than that day in the hospital.

It killed me knowing I gave up my baby without even looking at him. Without letting him know, even though he couldn't understand, how much I loved him and only wanted the best for him. I tried not to dwell on the past, because it was over and done, and nothing could change it. I had to live with myself and the decisions I'd made.

"Hey boss, there's a customer asking for you. She said you were holding a dress for her," Gina called out as she stuck her head in my office. I had been sitting at my desk, going through payroll and ruminating on this past weekend. Tossing my thoughts to the back burner, although I knew they'd resurface, I stepped out from behind my desk and headed out to help my client.

The day flew by as a steady stream of customers came in and left. When we finally locked the doors and put out the "Closed" sign, I sighed in resignation. I had delayed talking to Penny for too long. She was one of my best friends, if not *the* best, and I had been keeping secrets from her. Big secrets. The biggest of all being Alex. Connor was the only person, besides my dad, who knew about him.

I had also neglected to tell her about my encounter with Connor the other night, and I knew she was going to kill me. Not because I had been with Connor, or that it had taken me two days to tell her. She was always pushing me in his direction, and I continually resisted. The fact that I finally broke my own rule was going to have her saying "I told you so." No, she was going to kill me because she knew nothing of Alex. A secret of that magnitude would test the bonds of our friendship. I hoped it survived.

With Connor now out of the picture, I needed to find someone else who would help me. Sadly, I knew no one else, so I had no idea what I was going to do. I needed her to talk to Marcus for me. Surely, he knew someone besides Connor I could ask. I should probably go to the police, but what was I going to tell them? Hey, the baby I gave away for adoption might have called me out of the blue sounding desperate for aid. Can you please help me? I'm sure they'd get right on that.

I walked the short distance home, stopping briefly at the cafe two storefronts down to grab dinner. I took my time eating, avoiding the phone call I was dreading. After I finished my meal, I did everything else I could think of to procrastinate, including cleaning up an already clean kitchen and sweeping my floor. Eventually, I ran out of things to clean and knew the time had come to just call Penny and be done with it. I flopped onto the couch and curled my legs underneath me. I reached for my cell phone and, after searching my contacts, tapped Penny's name on the screen.

"Hey, you," she happily greeted me.

I figured I would say it for her. "I told you so."

"Huh? What are you talking about?" she asked, confusion evident in her tone.

"I figured I'd save you the breath and say it for you. I told you so."

"If you don't tell me what the hell you're talking about, I'm going to scream," she warned.

I coughed out, "I played with Connor at Eden."

I could almost hear her brain working, trying to decipher my words hidden in the coughing sound. I knew the minute she figured it out, because she screeched like a banshee in my ear.

"Oh my God, what? When?"

"Saturday night. It just happened. I was looking for you and saw him standing at the bar. Before I even knew what was happening, I walked over and started flirting. One thing led to another, and suddenly we were in one of the private rooms."

"I can't believe it finally happened. I've been waiting for this day. I knew you guys were perfect for each other. And the looks he sends your way when he doesn't think anyone is watching? Sigh. They're exactly the looks Marcus sends me. That man is head over heels in love with you. I'm so happy," she ended on a squeal of excitement.

"You might want to reel in the happiness. It was a one-time deal."

"What did you do?"

I couldn't help laughing, because she had me pegged. "Excuse me, bitch, but I would like to go on record that it wasn't me who rebuffed the guy this time. It was all that asshole Dom's fault. Everything was perfect before he fucked it up. I actually felt something. A connection. A spark I wanted to explore further. Which was the whole reason I never scened with him before in the first place. I knew it was going to end badly. Although, to be honest, I thought it would be his heart I broke. I didn't realize the power he had that could lead to it being my heart that was broken. I'm not saying he broke my heart. I'm just saying he could if I let myself get that involved."

She groaned softly in the background. "I'm so sorry, Bridget. I thought for sure you two were perfect for each other. I'm curious, though, how he fucked up. What happened?"

"Honestly, it doesn't really matter. We're done. There is something else though. I know it's late, but are you busy? Do you think you could come over? What I have to tell you is best said in person, no matter how much I don't want to face you when you find out."

"That sounds ominous. I'll have to double-check with Marcus, but it shouldn't be a problem. If it is, I'll call you back. Otherwise, I'll see you in about twenty minutes."

After saying our goodbyes, I hung up the phone and tried to keep myself busy while I waited for her to arrive. My condo was practically spotless by the time she got there. At the knock on the door, I let her in. She gave me a giant hug before making her way over to the couch. She took off her shoes before settling in.

Penny patted the spot on the sofa next to her. As I took my seat near her, she started speaking. "Okay, I'm waiting. What is so important that you needed to tell me face to face?"

Shit, I so wasn't ready for this. I took a deep breath, said a silent prayer she would forgive me, and dropped the same bomb I dropped on Connor.

"I have a son."

She blinked in response. Then nothing.

I fidgeted in nervousness. "Did you hear me? I said I have a son."

"I heard you. I'm processing. Give me a minute."

I sat back and stared at her. Nothing about her expression gave away what she was thinking. I hated this overwhelming nervousness. I wasn't that person. I always knew what I wanted, and I went after it. I didn't hesitate, and I didn't fucking fidget. A minute passed, then another.

I lost my patience. "Okay, you're done processing. Say something. Anything."

"What's his name?"

"Alex. He's gorgeous. He looks a little like me, I think. Auburn hair with brown eyes. And tall. He's thirteen, almost fourteen." I paused, a small, proud smile on my face as I thought of my son. "I know he likes baseball and football. And video games. He loves video games. His adoptive parents send me pictures and stories about him all the time. At least they did."

I trailed off, and the smile left my face. I stared off in the distance, the silence between us deafening.

Next to me, Penny cleared her throat. "Where is he now?"

Sadness poured out of me. "That's the thing. I don't know. A little over a week ago I received a phone call from a boy saying he thought I was his birth mother and that he needed help. Before the conversation could go any further, I heard noise in the background and then the line went dead. I didn't know what to do. So, I went to Connor. I told him everything I'm telling you. Two days after the first phone call, the boy called again and said he was Alex and that his adoptive parents were dead. He said he couldn't talk long because 'he' might come back. I have no idea who 'he' is, and it's killing me, because I haven't heard from him since."

I had to stop talking for a second, because I felt myself starting to become hysterical. Once my emotions were under control, I continued, "Then this thing happened with Connor, and I told him I didn't need his help anymore. But now, I don't know what to do. I don't know anyone else who could possibly help me. I know you're probably so pissed at me right now, but I was hoping maybe you could talk to Marcus for me. See if he knows anyone else I could turn to. I'm at a loss as to what to do. I can't keep sitting back, twiddling my thumbs, waiting. I need to do something."

Unable to control myself any longer, I burst into tears. The sofa dipped, and suddenly, Penny embraced me, and I cried for everything I had lost. Body-wracking sobs came from deep within me; I wasn't sure I would ever stop crying. I lost track of time as Penny comforted me. Eventually, my sobs subsided. I released my death grip on her and sat back on the couch. She leaned over and wiped a stray tear from my cheek.

She gave me a sad smile. "Feel any better?"

Actually, I did. "Yes," I said, with a watery smile. "You don't hate me do you?"

Penny smacked me on the arm. "Of course not. I'm a little hurt that you didn't trust me with this information before today, but I could never hate you. I'll ask Marcus if he knows anyone. But Bridge, honestly, I think Connor is going to be your best option. He's good at what he does. Personal feelings aside, I think you should reconsider."

I sighed heavily. "God, you're in a pain in the ass. Fine, I'll think about it. But, please, ask Marcus anyway."

She nodded her agreement. We let the topic go as Penny stayed a little longer and we caught up on some of the latest gossip. Finally, she left and I went to bed, contemplating the limited options I had.

CHAPTER 8

LIKE HOSPITALS, police stations have their own distinct smell. The scent of coffee, unwashed bodies, and even a slight hint of gunpowder, as though someone had just fired a gun, permeated the air. I stood inside the precinct and waited for Detective Daniel Webber to make an appearance. I dealt with the local authorities on occasion, but not frequently. The last time I, unfortunately, needed Webber's assistance was one night a few months ago. I'd been working on a protection case for my friend Marcus. I continued to live with the guilt that, had I done my job better, someone close to Marcus would still be alive. It was just another burden to add to my already weighed down shoulders. A burden I took full responsibility for.

After a twenty-minute wait, Detective Webber sidled out of what I assumed was his office toward me. He was young, about my age, with tanned skin and shaggy, light brown hair that looked like it belonged on a surfer from California. He had taken off his suit jacket, and I recognized the edges of two half-sleeve tattoos on each of his muscular upper arms beneath his rolled up sleeves. Interesting that I hadn't noticed them the last time we'd been in each other's presence. Of course, I'd been too busy cleaning up one of his fuck-ups to pay attention. When he stood close enough to reach out and shake my hand, I couldn't help the satisfaction I felt that I had to look slightly down my nose at him since he was shorter than my own six foot four frame.

"Mr. Black, I don't see much of you around here. What can I do for you?" he greeted me.

I glanced around before questioning him. "Is there somewhere private we can talk?"

Webber motioned me to follow him as we headed into the same office he'd just exited. After he directed me to a chair on one side of his desk, he took a seat in the chair opposite me, put his hands behind his head, and reclined, striking a far too relaxed pose.

"Now, would you like to tell me what this is about?" he asked, seemingly uninterested. For some reason, his entire attitude seemed fake. He was trying for nonchalance and failing. I wondered what his angle was.

"I'd like to preface this conversation with a promise that it goes no further than you and me. It's not my story to tell, and if she finds out I told you, she's going to be even more pissed at me than she already is. Plus, I have no proof beyond speculation." I began.

"She?" he queried.

"Do I have your word or not, Detective?" I snapped.

Webber sat forward in his chair, removing his hands from behind his head, only to hold them palm out toward me in a placating motion. "Okay, okay. Damn. Yes, only insofar as nothing you tell me breaks any laws or concerns breaking any laws. Now, talk."

I shared with him exactly what Bridget had shared with me. I told him about the phone call, and I told him about my encounters with Alex, including finding the handprint bruise around the boy's bicep, and the bullshit story he had tried to pass off on how he received it. I concluded with the information I had gathered during my reconnaissance about the regimental schedule Malcolm Shipman maintained and that something felt out of place. Then I sat there and waited as Webber digested the information.

After an eternity passed, he responded. "So, let me get this straight. Your girlfriend gives up a kid for adoption. He's now calling her for help for a reason no one can figure out. You find a bruise on him that could have actually happened in the exact way he described, but because he's your girlfriend's kid and his uncle has a regimental schedule, you think he's beating up on the boy? Do I have it right?"

I stood abruptly, almost knocking the chair backward in my haste. "Fuck you, Webber. I have a legitimate reason to believe Alex is being abused. Just because you can't get your head out of your ass to see it, doesn't make it false. If you aren't going to help me figure out how to help this kid, then you can kiss my ass. I'll do my job and yours. Thanks for wasting my time, asshole. I'll see myself out." I jerked an about-face and headed toward the door, understanding now why Bridget had come to me and not the police.

I had almost yanked the door off its hinges when a booming voice sounded behind me. "Black, get your ass back in here."

The offended SOB in me had me flipping the fucker off and storming away because I didn't follow commands, especially those given by some dickwad with a badge. The more rational part of my brain told me I needed to stop and turn around. I needed to play nice for Alex's sake. Luckily for everyone, I listened to the rational side. I slowly turned, jaw clenched to hold back the big "fuck you". It took all of my tightly held control to softly close the door behind me and walk back to the chair I had vacated seconds ago. I sat down and glared at the man across from me.

Webber sighed heavily. "Look, I didn't say I didn't believe you, but I can't start harassing a guy because of a single bruise you saw on some boy, regardless of who his mother is to you. These are serious allegations you are bringing up, and they need to be handled with care. Based on what you described, my gut is saying exactly what yours is. But neither of us can go off half-cocked because of a gut feeling. I need to tread lightly. My ass is already under scrutiny with another case I'm working on. I don't plan on getting fired because I fucked up again."

I was still pissed and could feel the vein throbbing in my temple. "To be honest, I don't give a shit about your ass. All I care about is this kid. You can either help me or not, but regardless, I'm going to do everything in my power to make sure that this abusive fuck is put away for a long time. Let this be fair warning to you, Detective. Tread lightly all you want, but I will destroy anyone who gets in my way of taking this motherfucker down. Are we clear?"

Webber stared at me for several minutes, neither of us breaking eye contact, before he finally answered. "Crystal. But let me be clear as well. What you do is your business, but it'll become mine if you break the law. Do that, and I'll be on your ass like flies on shit. Are *we* clear?"

With a nod, I stood as calmly as I could considering the anger I felt and walked out of his office making plans about what to do next.

CHAPTER 9

FRUSTRATION WAS NOT an emotion I handled well. I had been busy over the past three days researching different private investigators after Penny told me that Marcus didn't know of anyone else besides Connor who could help me. They both kept trying to cement the idea that Connor was my best option anyway. In my heart, I knew they were right, but damn it, I didn't want them to be.

It wasn't the expense; I wanted to find a reputable PI, but I didn't even know what kind of questions to ask to make sure I wasn't going to get hustled. I hadn't heard from Alex again, and it had been a week and a half. I wasn't sleeping at night, but there was nothing I could do right now.

I was helping a customer pick out an outfit for a blind date she was going on when the front door's overhead bell jingled. I was working alone today so I yelled out, "Welcome to Unique Boutique. Take a look around, and I'll be right with you." In the five years since I had taken over the store, we had only been shoplifted from once, so I didn't worry too much about who had entered the store.

After ten minutes of picking out this skirt to go with that blouse and a matching necklace to complete the outfit of the hardest-to-please customer I had dealt with in a while, we finally headed to the cash register. I only hoped the waiting patron wasn't too pissed about the delay. I drew to an abrupt halt upon seeing the person waiting by the front door, causing my customer to slam into my back with an oomph.

Mumbling an apology over my shoulder, I stumbled slightly as I continued walking over to the cash register. I tried to ignore the imposing man standing against the window with his arms crossed over his chest and one foot crossed over the other. Connor looked all too delicious in his dark-wash blue jeans and baby blue button-down shirt with the sleeves rolled up to his elbows exposing the ropey veins threading down his forearms.

I finished ringing up her purchases and then escorted the woman to the door as I wished her luck on her date. No sooner had she left than I felt Connor's heat radiating off him. He reached over my shoulder, flipped the "OPEN" sign to "CLOSED", and turned the lock on the door.

I turned toward him with a glare. "Whatever you have to say, make it quick. You're costing me money."

"First off, I'm sorry about what happened at Eden. Sec—"

"Are you sorry it happened or sorry you were such an asshole?" I interrupted, mimicking his earlier pose as I crossed my arms over my chest, because I knew the position pushed my boobs up. He needed to be reminded of what he was missing out on.

He took a deep breath and pinched the bridge of his nose, his frustration evident.

"Stop being a brat, Bridget."

I huffed, standing my ground. "Or what? You'll punish me? Take a crop to my ass until tears run down my face? You made your stance perfectly clear the other night, Connor. Now, say what you came here to say then leave so I can get back to work."

I knew I was being a brat, but somehow, after one night, I'd lost control of my emotions around him. I didn't know how to process the feelings I was having, because they were unexplainable. I had never experienced them before. Frankly, they needed to go away. Right now, the only way I could express them was by being a brat. They just exploded out of me.

Finally, Connor spoke again, reining in his frustration for the moment. "Like I said, I'm sorry about the other night. Regardless, I have no intention of giving up on helping you. You came to me because I'm good at what I do. We need to set aside personal conflicts and focus on what's important. Alex is who matters right now. I saw him, you know."

This had my total attention. I forgot about being pissed at Connor for a moment. "Oh my God, Connor, what did he say? Is he okay? Does he look all right? Is he safe?" I fired off question after question.

He reached out and lightly grasped my shoulders in his large hands. I ignored the zing that ripped through me. "He looks just like you and has the same ballsy attitude. His parents died a couple months ago, and he's been living with his uncle. He's skinny, but other than that, he looks fine. He doesn't seem to have any friends, but he's in a new neighborhood and probably hasn't had a chance to make any yet. I have a couple concerns that I addressed with an acquaintance of mine on the police for—"

"Police?" I interrupted, my voice loud with hysteria.

"What kind of concerns would you have that need the police, Connor? Tell me where he is, now! What is happening to my baby?" I screamed the last question, as I started punching Connor's chest, terror running through my veins at the thought that someone was hurting my child.

My outburst was abruptly silenced when Connor's lips crashed against mine with punishing force. I didn't have time to process the interruption as a rush of flavors burst across my tongue when his began to dance with mine, short circuiting my brain. He moved one hand from my shoulder and threaded his fingers through my hair before grabbing a fistful and pulling my head back to give him better access. Thankfully, I was tall, especially in heels, so I had no difficulty reaching up to meet him.

The kiss lasted for a lifetime as he drank from me and I from him. I almost felt my soul meld with his, as though we were now a part of each other. I shook off the image, and when I remembered why he'd distracted me, I pushed him away. As large as he was, he moved away with only the slightest push like he had been prepared for it.

We were both breathing heavy as we stared at each other. I tried desperately to read the expression in his eyes, but he shielded them, and there was no hope of busting through his defenses. "Have you calmed down, now?"

Hell no, I wasn't calm. Not in the way he meant anyway. I knew he was referring to my outburst about Alex. I took several deep breaths to slow my beating heart.

I backed up a few steps away from him and walked toward the interior of the store. "I'm fine. I apologize for hitting you. Now, please tell me what's going on." I practically begged, but far less hysterically than before.

I watched as Connor combed his fingers through his dark

wavy hair, mussing it in the process. "Like I said, I saw Alex. I met him while he waited for the school bus the other day. He moved past me to get to the bus, and when I touched his arm, he winced in pain."

I listened in rapt attention and gasped in horror. As I was about to say something, Connor placed his finger across my kiss-bruised lips and began speaking again, "He showed me a bruise and explained how he got it. It was a legitimate excuse, but something didn't ring true. I went to see a detective I know about it and to let him in on my suspicions. Unfortunately, there isn't much he can do until there is some actual evidence. Either eyewitness reports or Alex tells someone he is being hurt. I'm keeping an eye on him, Bridget. For now, I have to believe Alex told the truth and that he's safe. You have to trust me. I am not going to let anything happen to him."

He reached out again, this time cupping my cheeks. Slowly, he bent down and lightly brushed a kiss against my mouth. It was gentle and lasted but for only a heartbeat. It was a kiss of promise. A promise that nothing would harm me or mine.

CHAPTER 10

Based on my last conversation with Alex, I knew I wouldn't get anything further going that route. I needed to focus my attention on Malcolm Shipman. I needed to feel him out. Hone in on what kind of man he was. I left home a little early and headed to the gym he frequented. I had secured a guest pass during a previous visit, so I didn't have trouble getting in. I had just stepped on the treadmill when I saw him walk through the door. I watched as he headed to the elliptical machines. I hopped off the treadmill and jumped onto the elliptical right next to him.

After a couple minutes of fiddling with the machine as though I didn't know how to work it, I interrupted his workout.

"Hey, I hate to bother you, but how do you work this damn thing?" I asked, sheepishly.

He threw me an undisguised look of disgust. "You hit start."

I looked at the dashboard and a surprised, or so I hoped,

look came across my face. "Well, hell. What do you know? I didn't even see it there. Thanks, man."

I thought I heard the word "idiot" under his breath, but I ignored it. I'd made contact even if I had to look dumb doing it. I pumped away on the machine for twenty minutes without further conversation, even though Malcolm had left his machine five minutes earlier and was now lifting free weights on the other side of the gym. After finishing my cardio, I wiped down the machine and headed in his direction. I sat down on the bench press after loading the bar with weights and shelving it on the brackets above the bench.

"Hey, man, would you spot me?" I raised my voice to be heard over the din of voices and pulsing beats coming from the speakers in the ceiling. He either didn't hear me or was ignoring me, so I tried again.

"Excuse me. I'm sorry to bother you again, but would you help a brother out for a sec? I need a spot." I spoke a little louder this time. Finally, Malcolm turned his head to look at me. I maintained eye contact as I asked for the third time, "Spot me?" He looked around, maybe hoping for someone else to come to my aid. When none was forthcoming, he roughly dropped his weight and walked over, irritation in every step.

I stuck my hand out and introduced myself. "Thanks, brother. I appreciate it. I'm Connor."

Begrudgingly, he reached out and took it. "Malcolm." After a handshake I could tell he tried to put a little extra muscle into, he took his place at the head of the bench. I lay down on the bench, and after positioning myself where I felt comfortable, I reached above me for the bar. I had intentionally used less weight than I could comfortably press. After twelve of my fifteen reps I made a show of struggling with my upward press. Malcolm reached out to help me get the bar back to its bracket. When I made to initiate my next rep, he spoke.

"Look, I don't have time for this. You barely got the bar up the last time."

I put a confused look on my face. "Isn't that what you're here for? To spot me in case I need help?"

I sensed not only his irritation, but also frustration. "Well yeah, but you've barely lifted anything, and you're already tired. I have my own workout to get done. Next time, bring a friend to spot you." He walked away, his words an apparent dismissal, and went back to lifting his own weights. *Dick*. I removed the weights from the bench bar and stacked them back in their home and headed to the exit. I got what I'd come for, which was to discover at least something about Malcolm Shipman that a piece of paper wouldn't tell me. I imagined this wouldn't be my last time stopping in here.

After I left the gym, I headed back to the office to do some research. I sat at my desk going through all the paperwork I'd printed off about Malcolm and Alex Shipman. I wasn't sure exactly what I was looking for, but for the moment I was at a standstill. I hated it. I hated not being in control of things. I thought about Alex and his feeble excuse. Against my will, my mind wandered to another time and place.

"Please, stop. I promise I won't do it again," the little boy cried. He cowered in the corner, making himself as small as possible, as the echo of flesh meeting flesh reverberated through the room.

"How many times do I have to tell you to pick up your shit?" the man yelled, the odor of cigarettes and alcohol filling the room with each word he spoke. "I told you the last time I stepped on this

goddamn toy that I'd whip your ass if it happened again. You didn't listen. Now, stop being such a little pussy and take your punishment like a man. Stand up."

Gingerly, the boy rose from his crouched position on the floor. He sniffed back the tears. "I'm sorry, sir," he apologized.

"Turn around," the man ordered. Slowly, the boy gave his back to the man and waited in dread for what would happen next. A slight rustle of sound was heard behind him, followed by a single command. "Now, count."

At first, the boy stood confused as to what he was supposed to count. Until the blazing inferno of pain raced across his back and the slap of leather hitting flesh boomed in his ear. A scream of agony vibrated through the room. The room danced in front of the little boy's eyes.

"I said count, goddamn it," the man bellowed.

"One," the boy choked out. Before the boy could catch his next breath, another stabbing pain shot down his spine as the next slash of the leather belt and metal buckle hit.

"Two." On and on this went for eight more counts, the screams of pain bellowing throughout the house. Each strike weakened the boy until he was ready to collapse, but he stood tall and strong for as long as he could. Until finally, the boy could take it no longer, and at the count of ten he was brought to his knees.

A booted heel kicked at the boy's already battered back, forcing him to the ground, his voice only able to croak out a hoarse cry. He continued to lie there in tense anticipation of more agony. When none was forthcoming, he relaxed only slightly, not trusting the reprieve. A sound came from his left, and he slowly turned his head in dread. The man squatted next to him and took a swig from the bottle he had placed on the counter before the punishment began.

"Next time it'll be worse," the man warned. "Don't make me tell you again to pick up your fucking shit." He stood, making his *way over to the recliner where he sat and picked up the remote and the cigarette left burning in the ashtray next to it. He changed the channels, inhaling tar and nicotine, until a baseball game came across the screen. He became engrossed in the score, dismissing the boy who lay facedown, quivering in fear and pain.*

I didn't realize I was sweating until a droplet splattered on the paper in my hand. The scars across my back throbbed with the memory. The memories had been coming more frequently since seeing the bruises on Alex's arm. I thought of all the excuses that other pitiful little boy made for the abuse.

If only he'd picked up his toys.

If only he hadn't broken that dish.

If only he hadn't kicked the ball and busted out the tail light of the car.

If only he hadn't been born.

I snapped the pencil I'd been holding in half and threw it across the room in disgust. I was only more determined to find proof that Malcolm Shipman was an abusive bastard. Out of the corner of my eye, I caught the glimpse of something that caused my pulse to race in excitement. Something possibly monumental. I might have just found a motive for murder.

CHAPTER 11

It was early on Friday evening, and I sat on my couch watching television when my intercom buzzed. I wasn't expecting anyone so I ignored it. Within a few seconds, it buzzed again. Grudgingly, I got up and pushed the call button.

"Yes, can I help you?" I asked the person who likely hit the wrong button.

A deep, sexy voice crackled over the speaker in response. "Ms. Carter? My name is Detective Webber from the Pinegrove Police Department. May I come up? I'd like to speak with you."

Confusion ran through me. Why would the police want to speak to me? "I'm sorry, but what is this about?" Who knew if this guy was who he said he was. I couldn't be too cautious.

"I'd rather discuss it in private. You're welcome to contact Connor Black if you'd like to verify my identity." He must have sensed my hesitation.

What the hell? Upon hearing Connor's name, my heart

rate accelerated. Did this have something to do with Alex? Connor did say he'd spoken to a police acquaintance of his. Was that what this was about? Needing to find out, I was no longer hesitant.

"No, no. I'll buzz you in. Come on up." I released the speaker button and pressed the button the unlock the front door. Then I waited in anticipation for the knock, which came only moments later.

Stepping over to the door, I peeked out the peephole to see a gorgeous man in a suit standing there. I cracked open the door, leaving the security chain hooked, just in case.

"Yes?" I questioned.

He reached inside his suit and pulled out a wallet. He flipped it open, exposing the badge inside, and introduced himself again.

"Ms. Carter, I'm Detective Daniel Webber. Like I said, I spoke with Connor Black the other day, and I was hoping I could ask you a few questions. May I come in? I won't take up too much of your time."

"Yes, please, come in," I offered, closing the door only long enough to unhook the chain. I held the door open for him as he entered on a whiff of Old Spice, a scent I always found sexy on a man. "Now, can you tell me what this is about?"

He turned, and his eyes scanned my body from head to toe. I had been lounging around the house and hadn't been expecting company, so I was braless in a tank and short-shorts. It was a slow, almost sensual exam that actually had my body heating by the time his eyes met mine. I put my hands on my hips and tapped my foot. "If you're done eye-fucking me, can we move this conversation along?" I asked, bitingly. If this was about Alex, I didn't have time for this bullshit, no matter how hot the detective was.

He blinked, raised his eyebrows at my blunt words, and then threw his head back in laughter. "Oh, I like you. It's no wonder Black's afraid of you. You're a spitfire. I bet you keep him on his toes."

I huffed, "Look, Detective, no disrespect, but what the fuck do you want? If this is about Alex, quit dicking around and ask me your questions. This is my son's life you're being blasé about."

My words sobered him. "You're right, I apologize. Yes, I'd like to speak with you about Alex."

I nodded in acceptance of his apology. "You said you had questions for me. I'll tell you anything you need to know to help my son." I directed him to the living room where I offered him a seat and something to drink. He sat, but declined the drink.

"Black told me your story. I'd like to hear from you why you think your son is in danger," he stated, pulling out a notebook and pen from his inner suit pocket.

I took a seat on the other end of the couch and described both of the phone calls I received from Alex. "He sounded scared both times. And he hung up quickly the second time after mentioning that 'he' was coming. Alex said he couldn't be found talking to me or he would get in trouble. Why would he get in trouble for talking to me? I'm terrified, because I don't know where he is or what is happening to him. And then there's the bruise."

"How long has it been since you last heard from your son?" he asked.

"Almost two weeks." I watched as he scribbled on his notepad.

"He said nothing else to you except that he would get in trouble for talking to you?"

I shook my head. "Both of our conversations lasted less than two minutes. He whispered so softly during the second call that I almost had trouble hearing him. But he definitely sounded distressed when he hung up on me after he said someone was coming."

He looked up from his notepad. "You say he spoke softly. Are you sure you heard him correctly? Maybe he meant someone wanted to use the phone so he needed to go."

"That's not what he said, Detective," I snapped. "This is exactly why I didn't come to you guys in the first place. I knew you wouldn't take me seriously." I stood up and made my way to the door. I opened it in expectation of his departure. "If those are all the questions you have, you should probably go. I don't think you can help me."

I stood there impatiently, and irritated at this total waste of my time. He stood from the couch, put his notepad and pen away, withdrew something else from his pocket, and strode over to me. To my surprise, he reached up, swept my hair away from my face, and cupped my cheek in his large, but gentle, hand. He rubbed his thumb across my cheekbone as he spoke.

"I do believe you when you say your son needs help, Bridget. Sadly, as a police officer, my hands are tied until I can find proof that your son is in danger. But as a man who wants to see justice done, I'll do what I can, unofficially, for Alex. I can't make any promises, but I'll do my best."

He removed his hand from my face and reached down to clasp one of mine. He turned it over and placed something in it before closing my fingers around it.

"If you need me for anything, call me. I'll do whatever I

can to help you." He walked out the door I forgot I'd been holding open without a backward glance. A little stunned by his touch, I slowly closed the door, before turning around and falling slightly backward against it with a loud exhale. I felt a sharp stick to my palm and remembered he'd given me something. I opened my hand and unfolded the crumpled card he'd placed in it. I smoothed out the crinkled paper and studied the name, Detective D. Webber, and what was most likely his personal cell number.

Well, that was unexpected.

CHAPTER 12

SATURDAY MORNINGS WERE USUALLY SPENT MEETING Penny for brunch and then running errands. I had spent most of last night replaying my visit from Detective Daniel Webber. His touch had sent the tiniest spark through me. Nothing like the inferno I felt at Connor's touch, but enough to intrigue me. I didn't know if Daniel was into kink, and I hadn't had vanilla sex since my senior year of high school. I had no idea why I was even thinking about him anyway. He offered to help with Alex; that was it. I was reading too much into his caress.

I finished tidying up the house and headed out the door. I loved living this close to downtown, because I could walk everywhere. Today was the perfect fall day with the leaves only just starting to turn. It was my favorite time of year. I leisurely strolled down the sidewalk, taking in the birds chirping and smelling the scent of fresh-cut grass in the air. I turned the corner and headed into Miller's Cafe.

Miller's is a quaint little diner owned by Joe and Betty Miller, and has been open for over sixty years. Their food is plentiful and inexpensive. I headed toward our usual table mid-way to the back of the restaurant where Penny was already waiting for me. I slid into the chair across from her with my back to the door.

"You'll never guess what happened last night." I teased her.

She bounced a little excitedly in her chair waiting for the juicy gossip. "Did you and Connor finally boink?" She whispered the last word.

"Boink? Good lord, woman. Have I taught you nothing? I don't boink; I fuck. And no, Connor and I didn't 'boink'." I laughed. The elderly couple two tables away sent a dirty glare our way at my word choice. I didn't care. I cussed like a sailor; sue me. There weren't any children around so they needed to get over it.

"Apparently, Connor went to an acquaintance of his at the police with some concerns he had about Alex. This acquaintance, one deliciously gorgeous officer named Daniel Webber, came by my house last night. He left his card with his personal cell phone number, and I am not kidding when I tell you he totally eye-fucked me. I have to be honest and say I definitely wasn't upset about it, either. He's hot and I didn't see a ring on his finger. Not that that means anything nowadays."

I could tell she deflated a little at my words. I knew her heart was set on Connor and me getting together. I hated to keep dashing her hopes. I doubted anything would come from a mild flirtation with the sexy detective, but it didn't hurt anything. We were both single, or at least I assumed the detective was single since I hadn't spotted a ring, and I wasn't dead yet. I could certainly appreciate a handsome man.

"Why does Connor have concerns about Alex?" she asked in puzzlement.

"He found a bruise on Alex, and even though Alex gave a reasonable excuse, Connor wasn't taking any chances. He at least wanted the police to know in case it turns into something more. God, I pray it doesn't. Alex being abused would be another thing that's my fault."

Penny reached across the table and laid her hand over mine. "Bridget, you need to stop with the guilt. You did what was right for Alex at the time. You have no control over the universe. Sometimes bad things happen. They're no one's fault. They just are. Stop beating yourself up."

Neither of us spoke for a few minutes. I tried to stop the guilt, but it never went away. I didn't need to bring our day down with my depression, so I broke the silence by asking about her adopted daughter, Hailey. Instantly, the atmosphere changed as a look of joy spread across Penny's face.

We chatted for a while about Hailey and how she was still adjusting to the change of having a new stepmom. Penny also talked about wanting another baby. She loved and treated Hailey as though she'd given birth to her, but she also wanted a baby that was hers and Marcus'.

Our food came, and conversation slowed as we focused on our meal. I noticed, though, that Penny was continuously distracted by something at the front of the restaurant. As I was about to turn around to see what had her attention she discreetly pointed.

"I can't be sure, but there's a young boy who appears to be watching us. Brace yourself before you turn around, Bridget, because he looks just like you."

My heart rate accelerated at her words and my head

whipped around. Joy filled my heart at the sight of him. In both shock and awe, I could only whisper, "Alex."

He appeared startled for a moment before another expression, one I couldn't determine, flashed across his face. Without warning, he jumped up from his chair so quickly it toppled over behind him. Then he took off running out of the cafe. Confused and worried, I leapt out of my own chair and gave chase, screaming his name.

I had never been athletic, but I ran as fast as I could, yelling Alex's name as I followed him for several blocks, until fatigue and a stitch in my side started slowing me down. Damn, that kid was fast. I ran until I exhausted myself without getting any closer to catching up with him. Tears poured down my face. I had been so close. Why was he running from me? It didn't make any sense. Finally, I had to force myself to stop, and he disappeared out of my sight.

I collapsed in exhaustion against the side of the building. My legs were so weak I slid down to my butt, bringing my knees to my chest, and laid my head on my knees and cried. When I finally got myself under control, I trudged back to the restaurant where a worried Penny waited. I slid back in to my vacated seat. I'm sure I looked a mess with a flushed face and tear tracks down my cheeks, but I didn't care.

With concern in her voice Penny apologized that she might have spooked him. I waved off her concern and list-lessly returned to my meal. Not able to eat anymore, I pushed my food around on my plate. The remainder of our morning was spent in heavy silence. Finally, I gave up any pretense of enjoying myself any longer.

"I'm sorry, Penny, but I need to get out of here. I hate that I'm ruining our brunch, but I'm just not in the mood for socializing anymore."

I rose from my seat with Penny following suit. She moved around the table until she stood next to me then reached out to grasp my hand

"Don't you dare say you're sorry. Is there anything I can do, Bridge? I feel like this is all my fault." Penny asked, concern evident in her voice.

I only shook my head. "No, I'm sorry I wasn't good company today."

"I understand. So, what are you going to do now?" she asked.

I shrugged in indecision. "I need to call Connor. Or maybe Daniel. Someone needs to check on Alex. I have no idea why he ran. God, this is killing me."

We hugged our goodbyes, and I skipped running my errands. Instead, I walked home and sat, staring into space, debating who I should call. Connor or Daniel? It didn't take me long to figure it out. My heart knew long before my brain did. I reached for my phone and dialed the number.

CHAPTER 13

My entire day yesterday had been spent combing through all the paperwork I'd dug up on the Shipmans, and I'd found something intriguing. Because of Bridget's concerns for Alex, all my focus had been on Malcolm Shipman and the boy. I hadn't paid close enough attention to his parents. Based on what I could find, the Shipmans had a hefty bank account and an even heftier insurance policy in place before their deaths. Their primary beneficiary, of course, was Alex, but as he was a minor, a trustee had been assigned as a secondary beneficiary. A trustee who just happened to be Alex Shipman's uncle. That could explain the luxury car that the average Joe wouldn't be able to afford under normal circumstances.

I understood that a leap from child abuse to murder was a giant one, but I didn't plan on leaving any stone unturned when it came to this case. I needed to know everything. I left everything at the office yesterday in order to give my eyes a rest. I would start fresh looking over it all on Monday. Tonight I needed Eden. I also needed to see Bridget. It had been a few days since I left her standing in her store with my promise, and I'd forced myself to stay away.

My phone rang, and I looked at the caller ID. My brow furrowed when I saw Bridget's name flash across the screen. It was a weird coincidence since I was just thinking about her. Then I started to worry and wonder why she would be calling me on a Saturday afternoon, especially since she still wasn't totally pleased with me.

"Hello, Bridget." I greeted her.

"Connor, I just saw Alex," she responded, a tone of worry sounding in my ear. "He was at the cafe where Penny and I were eating brunch. She saw him sitting there watching us, but when I turned and called out his name, he took off. I tried to chase after him, yelling for him to stop, but I lost him. Why would he run? Connor, please, I need you to find him for me." By the time she finished speaking, she had become slightly distressed sounding.

"Bridget, calm down. It's okay. He was probably just curious about you." I tried to placate her.

"But why would he run? Like he was afraid of something? It doesn't make sense."

No, it didn't, but I didn't want to make her more frantic than she already sounded. I did my best to calm her down. "I don't know. Maybe he got nervous and panicked when you tried to talk to him. He freaked, not knowing what to say to you. Look, I'll go check on him if it makes you feel better."

Her tremulous voice made my heart ache. "Please, Connor. I need to know he's okay."

I rushed to reassure her, "I'll head over to the house now, okay?"

She sighed softly. "Thank you, Connor."

There was nothing I wouldn't do for this woman. "You're welcome. I'll let you know if I find anything out. I promise."

After I hung up, I drove over to Alex's house. All was quiet. I hung around for a while, waiting for I don't know what. I don't really know what I expected to find coming over here, but I needed to do it to reassure Bridget. I knew her nerves were shot. Mine were too. Because even though no sign of life came from the house, I had a bad feeling. I'd learned over the years not to ignore my gut. Knowing I wasn't going to learn anything, I left and would check on Alex on Monday. I'd let Bridget know that all was clear when I saw her tonight.

I ENTERED the club and felt the pulsing of the beats reverberate through my skin. I inhaled deeply the smell of sex and sweat. I scanned the room for any sign of luscious red hair. When I didn't spot her immediately, I sauntered over to the bar and ordered a scotch on the rocks. I pondered what I was going to say when I saw her next. I didn't have long to think about it, because on my next sweep, I spotted her entering the doorway across the room.

My cock hardened at the sight of her dressed in an underbust Kelly green corset with black piping around the edges and peek-a-boo lace covering her breasts. I could barely see the outline of her dark brown areolas and nipples. She also had on sheer black cheeky boy shorts that only enhanced her toned ass cheeks. Her long, gorgeous legs glowed in the dimmed lights, and her calf muscles were defined as she stood in black shoes I'd heard women call "fuck me pumps".

She proceeded into the common room and stepped over to a group of women that included Gina. The women began chatting, but Bridget's face looked wan, and I could see the slight tension lines around her mouth and eyes. I knew she was worried and trying her best to be social.

I quickly finished my scotch and was about to draw her away from the ladies to, hopefully, ease her burden about Alex a little. As I began to head over there, I stopped and frowned when a new face appeared in my vision. *What the fuck was he doing here?* Webber strolled in looking extremely uncomfortable as he took in his surroundings. I also noticed people staring at him in his out-of-place navy pinstriped suit. Clothing was optional in Eden so it wasn't typical to see a man fully dressed.

I observed him as he ambled further into the club. His gaze bounced back and forth between the St. Andrew's Cross on the stage and the rope rigging apparatus on the perpendicular wall.

His eyes widened in shock when the Dom on stage snapped the bullwhip toward the waiting sub strapped to the cross. He took a quick step forward like we wanted to inter-vene, but stopped himself. I almost took pity on him and was about to come to his rescue when his gaze honed in on Brid-get. He began walking toward her, a sudden confidence in his stride. When he reached the group of women, stopping just behind Bridget, they all stopped talking except her. When she realized every one was silent and staring at something behind her, she turned to see who or what had their attention.

Her eyes bugged out and her mouth dropped in shock when she spied Webber behind her. I had to give her credit for recovering quickly. I could tell introductions were being made, although I had no idea how they knew each other. Webber, I knew, was definitely not a member of the club. The question was, who invited him? It couldn't have been Bridget since she was as shocked as I was that he was here. I couldn't take not knowing what was going on and seeing him continue to stare at her with this intense expression on his face I refused to name.

I moved from my semi-leaning position against the bar and attempted, without success, to nonchalantly wander over in their direction. Several people tried to stop me to say hi, but with what I knew was a thunderous expression on my face, they changed their minds and judged it best to get out of my way. I reached the group and forced a smile.

"Ladies." I turned and glared at the interloper and ground out, "Webber."

He nodded in response with a smirk I wanted to wipe off with my fist. "Black, always a pleasure. Ms. Carter was just introducing me to the rest of these lovely women." He had the gall to place his hand on the small of her back.

I immediately saw red and glanced at Bridget, who was looking anywhere but at me. I also noticed she didn't move away from his touch. "I didn't realize you knew *Ms. Carter*. And what are you doing here? You're definitely not a member. I never pictured you as a Dominant. A submissive, on the other hand? That I could see." I knew I was being a jealous asshole, but this fucker, with his hands all over Bridget, was pissing me off.

He shrugged, unfazed by my barbs. "No, I'm not a member. Yet. I was invited by the friend of a friend actually. So I could check the place out. See what this kinky lifestyle is all about. Maybe find someone who could teach me a thing or two." He moved an infinitesimal degree closer to Bridget. *Oh, hell no.*

I wasn't sure, but I think I growled then. "Well, I'm sure Gina here would be happy to teach you a thing or two. Now, if you'll excuse me, I need to speak with Ms. Carter alone for a moment."

Bridget's head snapped in my direction at this, and finally, she met my eyes. I don't know what she saw in them, but she must have thought it was in her best interest to agree. "Daniel, it was a, um, pleasure to see you again. Maybe we can talk before you leave."

"She'll be busy until then," I ground out. When she opened her mouth to rebut my statement, I instructed a little sharper than I intended, "With me. Now, Bridget."

CHAPTER 14

I BRISTLED AT HIS TONE, but excused myself and started walking to one of the couches in the common area. Connor snatched my hand in his and pulled me along with him toward the rooms in the back. I attempted to tug my hand out of his, but he refused to loosen his grip so I gave up resisting. I didn't want to make a scene in public, but when we got to our destination, he would be getting an earful. His macho man attitude pissed me off. Besides, I needed to know what he'd found out about Alex.

A sense of déjà vu ran through me as I followed Connor into the second room on the right. I wondered if he'd chosen this room specifically, or if it was purely coincidental. Either way, I stood in the middle of the room like before.

"Strip," came the same command from behind me.

Unlike last time, I turned to face him, ignoring the command. "What the hell is wrong with you tonight? You were rude to Daniel."

"Daniel?" he asked in a low tone. "When the fuck did you meet *Daniel*?"

I crossed my arms over my chest and cocked my head showing him how unaffected I was by his question. "I met him last night when he came by my house. He wanted to ask me some questions about Alex and the phone calls I received from him. He said you spoke to him about the case."

He huffed in disgust. "I told him everything in confidence. He had no business coming to you about this. I told you I would take care of everything."

I stared at him in irritation. "He's with the police, Connor. He has every business coming to me if it involves helping my son. Jesus, you sound jealous or some—"

I stopped mid-sentence when I saw his cheeks flush at the word jealous. I gasped. "You are, aren't you? You're jealous of Daniel. Oh, this is rich. The big, bad Dom is jealous of the cop."

"I'm not jealous," he argued. "You're a sub, Bridget. It's who you are. You need dominance. I highly doubt Webber knows the first thing about the kink lifestyle."

"Who said anything about him dominating me? I just met him last night, for God's sake. And what does that have to do with anything? He wants to help me with Alex, not get in my pants."

Now, it was his turn to laugh. "You have to be kidding me, right? Of course he wants to get in your pants. He's a guy. Het guys want to get in a woman's pants. It's how we're wired."

I glared at him. "So, what you're telling me is that the only reason a man would be interested in me is to get in my pants? He might not want to actually have a conversation and get to know me? You know what, never mind. We're getting off topic here. Look, he offered to help. I'm taking all the help I can get. I don't care who offers it. I only care about

Alex. And you still haven't told me what you found out. He should be your first priority, not this irrational jealousy about Daniel. He is willing to help me. I think I'll go talk to him about seeing Alex. Go beat your chest somewhere else. I'm out of here."

I stepped to move past him when he grabbed my arm and jerked me around to face him. Without another word spoken, he slammed his mouth down on mine. He devoured my lips like I was his last meal and he would never get enough. The kiss went on forever, and I never wanted it to end.

He fisted my hair and roughly pulled my head back. My gasp was more of surprise than pain. Our eyes met, and I saw his had darkened to almost black with arousal. He was breathing heavy, and I realized my breathing matched his.

"I've let you get away with being a brat for too long, Bridget. It stops now. Do you understand?" he growled, his voice deepened with desire.

I half-heartedly struggled against his grip. Then, I did something that always got me in trouble. I opened my big, fat mouth. "Oh, yeah? What are you going to do about it?"

He laughed, low and deep, sending shivers down my spine. "I'm going to give you something to do with that mouth that will keep you quiet."

He kept his hand fisted in my hair holding me in place. My gaze dropped, and I followed the movement of his other hand as he slowly lowered his pants enough to pull out his cock. He guided me down to my knees so I knelt in front of him.

"Suck," he ordered.

I stared at the beautiful specimen of manhood in front of me and licked my lips. In my slowness to follow his command, he thrust his hips forward and pressed it against my mouth, pushing it open. "I said, suck."

My reflexes took over and I began sucking, hollowing my cheeks with each pass as he began thrusting in and out. He fisted both hands in my hair and controlled the speed of my bobbing head. He also pushed himself farther into my mouth, going deeper in my throat with each thrust until finally, I was deep-throating him. I sucked for everything I was worth, and when I ran out of breath the slight popping sound of him removing his cock from my mouth sounded in the room.

"Take a deep breath and be prepared to swallow everything I give you. You better not spill a single drop or there will be consequences."

I barely had time to inhale before he thrust back into my mouth, and he quickened his previously slow thrusts. I couldn't resist reaching up to cup his balls and only hoped he allowed it. When he didn't force me to remove my hand, I stroked and played with his sac as I took in his entire length. I felt his balls draw up under my touch and a few deep pumps later, his seed exploded down my throat. I swallowed it all down, working my throat feverishly so as not to miss any. When I drank the last drop, he pulled my head away from him.

"Now, strip. Don't make me tell you a third time."

I clumsily rose to my feet, almost on autopilot, and began removing my clothes. He observed me with hooded eyes as he finished removing his pants. When I stood naked he slung me over his shoulder like a sack of potatoes.

"Oomph," I exhaled as the breath left me.

He flung me onto the bed, and before I even settled, he was straddling me. He grabbed my hands, placing them above my head. He stared deep into my eyes and I was unable to look away.

"You're mine tonight, Bridget."

I shivered at his words. I ignored the sense of dread that sank deep in the pit of my stomach about how everything would change after tonight. Even though I thought I knew where this was leading physically, I knew the road it took me on emotionally would be vastly different than Connor's path. For him, this was about jealousy and anger. It was about showing me who was in charge. I knew and accepted it.

Yes, I could safeword my way out of it. He didn't know my specific word, but "Red" was almost universal, and I could use it if I needed to. We still had not discussed negotiations or limits. And that didn't look like it was going to change any time soon. Nothing was different, except a slight shift in my feelings for Connor since the last time we were in this room, and I knew this was going to end badly. Connor still hadn't made any effort to discover my wants or needs. He was too focused on his jealousy. I also knew this would be about him showing me that I couldn't handle what he dished out. Yeah, I definitely didn't see this turning out well for either of us.

CHAPTER 15

WHAT THE FUCK was I doing? Jealous rage clouded my vision when I saw her talking to Webber. Before the moment I dragged her toward this room, I had no intention of engaging her for anything more than to update her on Alex. But the minute that asswipe touched her, my control snapped. My only thought was to mark her as mine. I wanted to rub my come over every inch of her body, inside and out, so the world would know she belonged to me. *Whoa. Rein it in Black. She'll never belong to you.* Even if I could never have her for more than tonight, it wasn't going to stop me from my current course.

I maintained a single handhold on her hands, keeping them above her head, while I used my free hand to reach down and tweak her nipples. Her breath hitched and her body trembled with need. I stretched and reached into the stand next to the bed and pulled out padded wrist cuffs. I quickly adorned each of her wrists with one, taking care to keep them loose enough to avoid cutting off circulation.

Then, I attached them to a single chain hanging from the D-ring drilled into the wall above the headboard.

Once her arms were secure, I sat back and admired the perfection of Bridget's body. Breasts that fit right inside the palm of my hand. The hourglass shape of her waist flared out into hips just wide enough to cradle mine as I thrust into her. Her breasts rose and fell with each breath she took. Her nipples were the perfect shade of coral and small like blueberries. I was dying for a taste. Unable to control myself any longer, I leaned forward and pulled one succulent tip into my mouth. Her back arched, pushing her breast further into my mouth. I pulled back and her nipple slipped out of my mouth with a little pop.

Not wanting to neglect the other breast, I focused my attention on it. I flicked my tongue across the pebbled berry, earning a moan from her. When Bridget again arched to push herself closer I pulled away and slapped her breast, causing it to pinken, and her to gasp.

"Lie still," I commanded. "Don't move again. Do you understand?"

She groaned in frustration, but nodded. "Yes, Sir."

I couldn't wait to sink my cock so deep inside her. I hadn't even realized how much I wanted this until Bridget lay spread out before me, a feast just waiting for me to dine. My mouth watered at the remembered taste of her. Like the sweetest of berries. And now she was at my mercy. I took one more lingering look before I stood and headed to the drawers built into the wall on the other side of the room. Her gaze followed my movements and her breathing sounded heavy in the air.

After gathering the implements I wanted, I returned back

to where Bridget waited. I set the two small pieces on the bed.

"I think your nipples need a little decoration."

I drew one nipple into my mouth, suckling it to a firm peak. I placed a rubber tipped nipple clamp on the tip, tightening the screw only slightly. I repeated the process with the other one. Then I tweaked each clamp.

"Breathe," I commanded as I tightened each screw more.

"Oh, god, enough," she pleaded.

I made another half turn. "You can take a little more, Bridget." I sat back and admired the beauty before me. She writhed from the sensation as I tugged the chain between the clamps.

I tugged again, but this time I circled her clit with my thumb. "Pain and pleasure are interchangeable. You feel the bite of the pain, but the pleasure is also there." I lowered my head, and as I continued circling her clit with my thumb, I swiped my tongue up her slit, sweeping up her flavor. I continued my oral assault and plunged my tongue deep inside her weeping hole. When she least expected it, I would tug the chain, pulling a little harder each time. Pain and pleasure collided each time until I knew she couldn't distinguish between the two. With a final tug, she screamed out her orgasm and her pussy spasmed around my tongue.

As tremors still racked her body, I loosened the first clamp and Bridget screamed as the blood rushed back into her nipple. I soothed the pain with my tongue. When I reached for the other, her head shook back and forth. "No, Sir, please. God, the pain."

"This is only a small taste of what I want to do to you, Bridget. You told me that you were never one to pass on a dare. I'm daring you to do this. No, that's not true. You *will* do this." Without giving her another chance to argue, I removed the second clamp, causing a cry of pain to escape. I chased it away again by surrounding her breast with the heat of my mouth. I laved her nipple, swirling my tongue around it. Slowly, I peppered kisses from her breasts, down to her stomach, and her inner thighs, avoiding the single spot where I knew she wanted my mouth the most.

When she arched to try and bring me in contact with her throbbing, wet cunt, I slapped her clit. She cried out from the pain.

"Don't forget who's in charge, Bridget. I'll touch you where I want when I want. This pussy is mine to do with as I please."

She groaned in frustration. I slapped her pussy again to bring her to attention. "Don't make me punish you."

"Yes, Sir." Her voice sounded pained. To drive my point home, I brushed kisses down the length of each leg, around each toe, and up her calf and inner thigh, continuing to bypass her center. I traveled upward again, dropping kisses across her shoulders, fingers, eyes, and her mouth. Everywhere but her throbbing core.

Eventually, I took pity on her and ran a single finger up and down her wet slit, swirling it around her clit before dropping it back down to trace her pussy entrance. I dipped the tip of my finger in to tease her. In and out I pressed, going deeper with each thrust. I added a second finger, then a third. I continued to finger fuck her, her cunt clenching on them with each push, trying to draw them further inside.

"You will not come until I tell you to. Do you hear me?"

Her head thrashed back and forth, the sweet agony of arousal crossing her face. When she didn't answer me, I reached up with my free hand and pinched her nipple between thumb and forefinger. Hard.

"I asked you a question."

"Yes, Sir, I will not come yet," she hissed, her teeth clenched in pain. I released her nipple with her answer and soothed it with my tongue. Wet slapping sounds continued as I kept up the thrusting of my fingers. I lowered my head until I was even with her clit and began flicking it with the tip of my tongue. I felt the beginning spasms begin deep inside her pussy. I withdrew all my fingers, and she groaned in frustration. I knew she'd been close to coming. I quickly donned the condom I'd also grabbed from a drawer

She was breathing heavy as if she'd just run a race. I knew my heart was racing as well. I couldn't hold out any longer. I shifted positions again, and before she could guess my intentions, I plunged my throbbing cock deep inside her. I fucked her with everything I had. My entire body screamed in ecstasy at finally being inside her. I had dreamed of this moment for far too long. The reality was so much better than any fantasy I'd ever had. I knew I wouldn't last long.

I reached down and rubbed her clit in a coordinated dance as I continued thrusting. Her pussy squeezed my cock, causing a groan to escape me. Our bodies meshed together to become one, our heartbeats synchronized, and a feeling of rightness came over me. So much so that I couldn't stop the feeling that rushed over me. The feeling that I could let the beast out. I still needed to keep him under control, but he needed a taste of more. I powered into her and increased the friction on her clit. Slapping flesh sounded and her pussy spasmed so hard I knew she was on the edge.

"Come for me, now, Bridget."

Her back arched as powerful tremors shook her entire

body with the force of her orgasm. Before she could recover, I flipped her over, roughly pulled her up onto her knees and moved her hands to the headboard to grab a handhold before immediately plunging my cock back into her pussy. I grabbed her hair and jerked her head back for more leverage, and without missing a beat, I began my punishing thrusts, pushing my length as deeply into her cunt as I could get.

"I told you before I would fuck you so hard and deep you wouldn't know where you ended and I began. You'll take every inch of my cock, Bridget. I'm going to come all over you and mark you so you'll know who you belong to."

Bridget met my brutal fucking stroke for stroke as she pushed back against me with each forward movement. A slapping sound reverberated through the room as our bodies came together.

"Yes, Sir. Fuck me. Mark me. I'm yours to do with whatever you choose." Her words spurred me on, and I rode her even harder. She continued to take everything I gave her. I pulled her up so her back met my front. I didn't think I could sink any deeper into her pussy than I already was, but this new position opened her up even more, and she gasped as she took in my entire length. I continued my assault as I reached around to finger her clit with one hand, and pinched a still sensitive nipple with the other.

The tremors began, and with only a single touch, she screamed "Sir" as she orgasmed again, this time around my cock, which then triggered mine. As I exploded inside her, it only seemed natural for me to bite down on that sensitive spot between her neck and shoulder, causing her body to spasm even more as her orgasm intensified.

As her body continued to tremble, I released my grip on

her, unlatched the wrist cuffs she still wore, and she collapsed forward onto her forearms in exhaustion, almost purring in satisfaction from another powerful orgasm. I remained half hard inside her. I shifted a little before finally pulling out. I hurriedly disposed of the condom and returned to the bed. Bridget rolled to her side and looked over at me.

"Thank you, Sir."

I lay down next to her face-to-face and pushed her sweat-dampened hair out of her eyes. Our gazes locked, and a thousand unspoken words passed between us. Neither of us wanted to break the spell we were both currently under. She reached out and plucked at the shirt I still wore. I clasped her hand in mine stopping the movement.

Her gaze drew up to mine, and I saw the question forming behind her eyes. I knew, inevitably, I was going to have to answer it. But I wanted to put it off as long as possible.

"This is twice now that we've been together and I still haven't seen what's underneath the clothing. I want, no, I need to touch you, Sir. I need that connection. I crave touch and textures. I want to learn what pleases you. Don't get me wrong; I loved everything you did to me. But, Sir, I don't know if that's enough. I'm not trying to be bratty or top from the bottom when I say this, but it's your job as a Dom to take care of me."

"And you don't think I've taken care of you?"

Her gaze dropped from mine and she stared at my chest. "I didn't say that, Sir. We haven't done anything by conventional means. I know tonight started out because you were jealous of Dan— I mean, Detective Webber, but it changed somewhere along the line. We both know it to be true, so please don't bother to deny it. But here's the thing. Despite that change, we still haven't really communicated. Not verbally, at least. You've been in this lifestyle long enough to know that communication is the basis of a D/s relationship. I feel like I'm in limbo. I want to please you, but I can't do that if I don't know what you expect of me. But you also need to know there are things I need. Things that make me who I am.

"I have always kept my encounters with other Doms superficial and for fun. It's a time where I don't have to be in control. I can let go. I like them well enough and certainly enjoyed the pleasure they've given me. But that's it. I've never felt a strong connection to any of them or wanted to explore something further with any of them."

She shifted, almost nervously, and her attention remained below eye-level. "And I can't believe I'm saying this, because I swore I never would, but I want to explore whatever this is with you. For me, that means more. It can't stay superficial and for fun. If I'm opening myself up to someone, to you, I need that reciprocated. It's how I'm wired."

I studied her a little longer and thought about what she'd said. I had a shitty childhood I fought tooth and nail to forget even if the scars that decorated by body refused to allow that to happen. To be vulnerable again sent chills through my body. It was as though I was reliving the helplessness all over again. I knew I was being irrational, but I had been conditioned from an early age that being vulnerable was a sign of weakness. It's what got me broken bones and burn scars over a quarter of my body. Just remembering it brought bile rising to the back of my throat, but I swallowed it down. Was I ready for what Bridget was asking of me? Hell, no. But if I didn't bite the bullet now, would I ever? I knew she would be worth it in the end though.

I tilted her chin up until her eyes met mine. "I want more too, Bridget. This is new to both of us, so we'll have to learn together. Since we're talking about needs, then let me tell you what I need. Your patience. It's not easy for me to be vulnerable to someone. I've always taken care of the subs I've played with. But I've never felt for any of them what I feel for you. Just give me some time."

Even though I knew it wasn't what she wanted to hear, she acquiesced. We remained lying together for a little while longer, each of us lost in our own thoughts.

CHAPTER 16

It was early Sunday afternoon, and I had been lounging around the house with thoughts of Bridget running through my head. I wanted to explore whatever we might have, but damned if I didn't break out in a cold sweat thinking about it. I knew she wanted me as much as I wanted her, but every time I thought about her seeing my scars, I cringed. God, I was such an emotional fucking pussy.

Not wanting to think about my scars and her potential rejection, I switched my train of thought back to Alex. I made the occasional drive-by over the last couple of days to check on him, including the one yesterday, but I was beginning to believe that there was some truth to his story about the bruises. I knew his routine by heart, and nothing had changed. I was pulled from my musings by the ringing of my personal cell phone.

"Connor Black."

A soft groan sounded on the other end. "Hello," I answered again.

"Mr. — Mr. Black," the young voice responded.

I bolted upright and swung my legs over the side of the couch. "Alex? What's wrong?"

I heard another pained moan. "Sir, I need your help. Can you come get me?"

Jumping up, I quickly began gathering my wallet, gun, and car keys. "Where are you, son?"

I could hear his heavy breathing. "I'm down the street from home at the library. They let me use their phone. Please, hurry."

I raced out of the house and into my car, breaking every speed limit rushing to get to Alex. Tires squealed as I pulled into the parking lot and found the closest open spot. I rushed inside, searching for him, hurrying down each aisle until I spotted him against the back wall, looking uncomfortable sitting on a cushioned chair. There were tear tracks on his face.

"Alex," I said softly, trying not to startle him. He jerked at the sound of my voice. He turned his head toward me and, as soon as he made eye contact, tears began flowing down his cheeks. I quickly scanned him from head to toe, but other than the tears and a wince when he shifted positions, nothing was different about his appearance. I moved over to where he sat and dropped into the chair next to him.

"What's wrong?" I asked, gently.

He sniffed and wiped his runny nose against the back of his hand, which he then rubbed across his pant leg. He took his time answering.

"I think my ribs are cracked. It hurts to breathe." He shifted again, wincing in the process. The tears came faster.

I didn't want to jump to conclusions, but I had a feeling I wasn't going to like what he had to tell me. I opened and closed my hands to ease the ache that had settled in while I clenched my fists through his telling. My jaw ached from being clenched as well, so I wiggled it back and forth to ease the tension. "I need to take you to the hospital. On the way there, you can tell me what happened."

"No," he yelled, then lowered his voice. "I can't go to the hospital. Can't you just wrap them or something? It's not like there is anything the hospital can do that you can't."

I didn't want to know how he knew that. "Alex, you might have some internal bleeding. Your rib could puncture your lung. You need to see a doctor."

He vehemently shook his head. "I told you, I can't go to the hospital. If I was bleeding, I'd know. You said I could trust you. That you would help me." He stared at me, waiting. He was right. I did say I would help him, but I struggled with making the right decision. He got tired of waiting and shook his head in disgust. "Never mind, I knew I shouldn't have called you."

He moved to stand up and gasped at the pain. He stood there for a second as he breathed through it. It was then that I made my choice.

"C'mon." I stood from my perch and put my hand on his shoulder.

He shrugged it off and grunted. "I told you, I'm not going to the hospital."

"I'm not taking you to the hospital. We're going to my house. Let's go."

He stared, hesitant in believing my words. When I sensed his indecision, I tried again to put my hand on his shoulder. This time, he remained still.

"I said I would help you, and I will. But we can't do it here. Now, are you coming or not?" I left it up to him. I could almost see the wheels turning in his head as he weighed his decision. With a short nod of acquiescence, he walked toward the front of the library and the exit.

Once outside, I pointed toward my car. Alex slowly lowered himself into the passenger seat and buckled his seat belt. I got behind the wheel and began the trek to my house. I didn't push him to explain what happened. At least not until we got home. Once we arrived, I ushered him inside and directed him to the living room. I left him there as I went to the medicine cabinet to get the Ace bandages. Five minutes later, he still stood in the middle of the room.

"Take off your shirt so I can get you wrapped." I instructed him.

Gingerly, he removed his shirt and tossed it on the love seat in front of the fireplace. I studied the mottled bruising along his left side that wrapped around toward the front and back of his torso. I gritted my teeth in fury. I knelt next to him and began the arduous process of binding his ribs. He hissed in pain I could relate to. I'd had many broken ribs in my childhood. A memory threatened, but I pushed it away.

I painstakingly completed the task, trying to cause the least amount of pain as possible. Once done, he painstakingly sat on the couch while I went to the kitchen to get him something to drink and some ibuprofen. Once he'd emptied the glass I set it on the coffee table. I sat on the edge of the recliner next to him, leaning forward with my elbows resting on my thighs and my chin resting on steepled fingers. Then I stared at him until he grew uncomfortable by my scrutiny.

"Now, tell me what happened."

I waited patiently for him to begin. Softly, he began speaking. "I thought I was careful, but he must have followed me. I wanted to see her up close. Just once. I needed to know what she looked like, and if I looked like her. I told him I was going to the library, but I found some money he'd hidden, and I took the city bus into town. I walked around asking people where her street was until I found where she lived. Her address was in the papers I discovered after my parents died."

My heart stopped at his words. He had to mean Bridget. I had a feeling this was going to be a long story. He took a shallow breath and continued. "I saw her leave, and she started walking toward downtown, so I followed her to this diner. I still had a little money left from the bus fare so I went in. She met a woman inside. I watched them for a while. Her friend kept glancing at me and finally pointed in my direction. She turned, and when she saw me, her eyes got wide, and I think she said my name. I only saw her mouth move. I got scared and ran. She followed me, but I'm fast. I could hear her screaming my name, but I panicked. I didn't know what to do. He said he would hurt her. I didn't mean for her to see me. I swear."

When he paused with his story, I got up and refilled his glass of water. When I heard Malcolm had threatened Bridget I needed to control my fury. I didn't want to scare the kid with the rage coursing through me. I'm sure my expression was ferocious. Once I had my rage under control, I brought Alex's water out to him. He licked his lips before guzzling the liquid down. He kept hold of the glass and fiddled with it in his hands turning it first one way then the other. He took a deep breath and kept going.

"I raced all the way to the bus stop and caught the next bus home. When I got there he was waiting for me. He began questioning where I had been. I tried explaining I was at the library. He slapped me across the face and told me not to lie to him. He was so angry. He yelled at me that I was to stay away from her or we'd both be sorry. He grabbed me, I lost my balance, and fell to the floor. Then he began kicking me. I begged him to stop, but he didn't listen. He just kept kicking. I curled into a ball, but it didn't help. I lost track of time, but finally he stopped.

"When he was done, he walked into the living room like nothing had happened and just left me laying there. When the pain eased, I picked myself up off the floor and went to my room. I stayed there all night, hoping the pain would go away. I still hurt when I woke up this morning. I waited until he left, walked to the library, and called you."

I had to keep my anger in check for the kid's sake. I wanted to punch my hand through the wall. This kid, no kid, deserved abuse such as this. I needed Webber to come see Alex.

"Alex, I need you to talk to a friend of mine." I told him.

"Who?" he asked hesitantly.

I knew this wasn't going to go over well, but it needed to be said. "His name is Daniel. He's a police officer with the Pinegrove Police. He —"

He interrupted me with a sharp shake of his head. "Hell no. You can't call the cops. He said he'd hurt her. I gotta go. I'm going to be in so much trouble."

Rage filled me at the thought of Bridget being threatened. "Alex, stop. Let us help you. He won't hurt her. I promise. I'll take care of her. But we need to talk to my friend." I waited patiently as he weighed my words. I needed to get him to talk to Webber. Finally, with a slight nod, he agreed. I pulled out my phone and dialed the number.

CHAPTER 17

ALEX and I sat in the living room waiting for Webber to show up. While we waited, Alex asked me questions about Bridget. He wanted to know everything about her. I knew these were things he needed to hear from her, so I only told him superficial things. They could talk about the deeper stuff later when they finally met. I needed to arrange a meeting between them. I would figure out how to deal with Malcolm. Because this fucker was going down. Some way, somehow.

Thirty minutes later, the doorbell rang. I left Alex sitting on the couch as I went down the hall to answer it. I let Webber in and shared what Alex told me. I saw him clench his fists in anger. I knew the feeling. We headed back into the living room where Alex waited.

"Alex, this is Daniel."

Alex still seemed a little belligerent about having to speak to the police, but he accepted the handshake Webber offered.

"It's nice to meet you, Alex. Connor here filled me in a

little on what happened, but I'd like to hear it in your own words." Webber spoke softly and coaxingly.

For the next thirty minutes, Alex repeated the story of traveling to see Bridget and the beating he'd received upon his return home. Webber had pulled a notepad and pen from his suit jacket before Alex had started his re-telling, and on occasion, the detective would jot things down as Alex spoke. At one point, he asked Alex to lift his shirt to see the bruises so he could take pictures of them with his phone. Most of them were covered with the ace wrap I used to bind his ribs, but there were still some that were prevalent around the edges. When he was finished speaking, he sank painfully into the couch, exhaustion taking its toll on his already battered body.

Webber looked at me, and with an almost imperceptible nod, he communicated he wanted to speak to me alone.

I looked over at Alex. Fatigue and pain lined his face. "Why don't you lie down for a little while, kid. We'll be right back."

He nodded and slowly lay down, closing his eyes with an exhausted, pained sigh.

I escorted Webber into the kitchen and leaned against the counter, waiting on what he had to say.

"So? What happens now?" I asked.

"With those bruises and with Alex's testimony, I can open an investigation. The problem is, I'm worried about Alex. Once I open a case, Alex will be removed from the home while it's conducted. Child Protective Services will be called in, and he will be assigned a social worker. They'll see if there is another family member who can take him in. If not, the state will take temporary custody of him, and his social worker will find a foster home for him until Mr. Shipman is cleared of any wrongdoing.

"We'll interview neighbors, co-workers, Alex's school, and anyone else that might corroborate Alex's story. If we can't find any substantial evidence to arrest Mr. Shipman, Alex will be returned to his care. If Mr. Shipman is abusing Alex, then the abuse will just start over, only this time, he'll take more care to hide it. I'm also concerned about the apparent threats that Shipman is making against Bridget. He could go after her, you know. Are you willing to take that risk?"

I studied Webber for a minute. I could see how Bridget would find him attractive. He was good-looking, had a successful career, and was probably a nice guy. But he couldn't give her what she needed. I didn't know if I could either, but damned if I didn't want to try.

"You let me worry about Bridget. I'll make sure she's taken care of."

He smirked at me. "Yes, I'm sure you'll try. But know this. I'll be waiting in the background, ready to pull up your slack. If she needs a shoulder to cry on when you let her down, I'll be there. Just because I don't know much about the lifestyle doesn't mean I wouldn't be a willing student were she to offer to teach me."

Neither of us broke eye contact, and it appeared the pissing contest was back on in full-force. There was no way I was going to concede to this cocky bastard. There was also no way that Bridget would ever be happy in a vanilla relationship. I felt a minimal amount of relief at that thought. I stood from my position against the counter and walked past him back into the living room with a little nudge to his shoulder as I passed. Right now my concern was for Alex.

Alex was asleep when we returned. I just looked at him, seeing Bridget in all of his features. They needed to meet. It was past time. Since there was really nothing more to discuss with Webber, I escorted him out. He promised to be in touch after he spoke to his boss about the investigation.

I let Alex sleep for a little bit. When I accidentally made too much noise, his eyes shot open, and his gaze darted around as he tried to orient himself to his surroundings. When his glance landed on me, he relaxed.

"Sorry I fell asleep. How long have I been out? Did Mr. Webber leave?" he questioned.

"Yeah, he left about thirty minutes ago. Don't worry about it. It looks like you needed the rest anyway." I reassured him.

"What time is it? I can't be gone much longer." He sounded nervous.

"I'll give you a ride home in a minute. First, we need to talk about something."

Considering the bomb I'd dropped by bringing the cop here, the leery expression on his face was justified. "Now what?"

"You need to meet Bridget face to face. No more phone calls. No more spying and running. You're hurting her, and she doesn't deserve it. You need to start growing up."

He hung his head, shamefaced. I let him absorb my words while I waited patiently for him to make his decision. I saw when he did.

"Okay. When?"

I silently congratulated him on making the right choice. "Let me talk to her. Arrange a meeting. She's been dying to know what is going on with you and wants to make sure you're all right. I told her about the bruise on your arm, but I think we need to keep this other thing between us. She doesn't need one more thing to worry about. Especially when there is nothing she can do about it. We clear?"

He nodded in understanding. "Yes, sir. We're clear."

"Good. Now, I'll take you back to the library. Then, I'll follow you home and make sure you're safe when you get there. I'll hang out for a little bit. If something happens, I'll be there."

He sagged in relief. "Thank you."

On the drive back to the library, I let him know I'd be in touch with him about the meeting with Bridget.

"Also, Webber will begin an investigation into the abuse. While he's investigating, you'll need to be removed from your uncle's house. They'll probably either place you in a group home or a foster home until they've finished asking neighbors, friends, and teachers if they have seen anything or suspect anything. I don't know how long the investigation will last."

Alex's head whipped around and he ground out a sound of disgust. "Do you have any idea what you've done? He's going to kill me or my mom now! Don't you understand what I've been trying to tell you? He threatened to kill both of us if I told anyone. And there is no chance anyone would be able to tell the police anything. God, this is pointless and a waste of time to try and do anything about it. You're only making my life, and hers, worse. I never should have called you."

He refused to speak to or even look at me the rest of the drive. He had his seatbelt unbuckled and jumped out of the car, cradling his ribs, clearly in pain, before I could even come to a complete stop.

"Just leave me alone." He started walking in the direction of his house.

I thought about calling him back, but there wasn't anything I could say to him to make him feel better, so I did the only thing I could. I slowly followed behind him as he made his way home. Once he got inside, I waited in my car down the block to make sure he didn't need me, even though I noticed Malcolm's car was missing. After an hour passed and Malcolm hadn't returned, I left and hoped for the best. The threat of the investigation was leverage Alex could use if things got out of hand. He was a smart enough kid; he wouldn't hesitate to use it.

CHAPTER 18

IT HAD BEEN the week from hell. I spent almost every day since Monday with the mother of all headaches. It all started on Sunday evening when Connor called and even though I pushed as hard as I could, he refused to tell me what Alex's uncle was being investigated for. Then, on Monday evening, I got a call from my security company about an alarm going off at the store. Police had been dispatched when the security monitors showed someone had tried to break in through the back door. I met the police there to make sure that nothing had been stolen.

On Wednesday night, someone had thrown a brick through the front window so I had to close up shop for the next two days while it was being replaced. I'd barely slept a wink all week, especially after the phone call from Connor, who I hadn't seen since Eden last Saturday.

I was stressed beyond my limit, and any second now, I was going to break. Not that I didn't want to meet Alex, but I was so nervous. What would we talk about? How would I explain to him my reasons for giving him up?

We had decided on a neutral place for the meeting so we chose the city park. I got there an hour early but was a ball of nervous energy, and I couldn't sit still. I traveled from one bench to the swings, back to another bench. I sat for five minutes before I bounced back to the swings. I sat in one and kicked my legs to propel me further in the air. Back and forth I swung, thinking about how my life would be different if I had kept Alex. I don't know why I tortured myself with coulda, woulda, shoulda, but the thoughts snuck up on me at least once every few days.

I was on a downward swing when I spotted them. I dug my heels into the ground to stop my momentum and brought myself to a halt. I stood up from the swing, and as they got closer, I braced myself for the first good look at my son. Pictures weren't the same as seeing someone in the flesh, and he'd dashed away so quickly at the restaurant that I never got a great look. After what felt like an eternity, they reached the place I stood. We all stood there, the tension so thick I could have cut it with a knife. I ran my gaze up and down Alex, memorizing everything about him. My whole body was shaking.

Connor was the one to finally break the silence. "Alex, this is Bridget."

He gave a shy smile and little wave. "Hi."

Tears threatened, but I tried to hold them back. I returned his smile with a watery smile of my own. "Hi. It's nice to meet you, Alex." I was suddenly self-conscious and drew a blank on what to say next. *Oh, God, he's going to hate me. I don't even know what to say to my own son.*

Again, Connor saved the day. "Maybe you guys could go sit over there and talk. Get to know each other." He pointed to the closest park bench surrounded by colorful flowers and greenery.

Alex shrugged and headed over there. I was a little slow to follow. Connor touched my arm. "Relax. He's nervous too, you know. Talk to him like a normal kid. Ask him about school, his hobbies. Don't worry about getting too deep today unless he wants to. Just get to know each other. You'll be fine." He bussed a light kiss on my cheek and swatted me on the butt to get me moving.

His words and the swat were the kick in the pants I needed. This meek and mild person was not who I was. I was strong. I could do this.

Alex had already taken a seat on the bench so I sat down next to him. Connor left us alone, but still remained in sight. I looked over at Alex and wondered what he was thinking. "I bet you have a lot of questions for me." Nothing like breaking the ice.

He drew designs in the dirt with his toes and shrugged. "Yeah, I guess."

Wow, this was harder than I thought. "Feel free to ask. I'll try to answer as honestly as I can."

He didn't say anything for a minute. I could tell he was forming a question. "Why?"

And there it was. The million dollar question. I assumed he meant why I gave him up. "Why did I give you up for adoption?" I clarified, just to make sure we were on the same page.

He nodded tightly.

I took a deep breath and gave him the best explanation I could. Nothing like getting the hard stuff out of the way first, I guess. "My mom died when I was seven. From then on, it was just my dad and me. He wanted to do everything he could to provide me with the things I needed, so he worked two jobs. I rarely saw him. The neighbor lady watched me a lot while he was always working. We were close even though I was a little resentful that we never got to spend a lot of time together. This continued until I was old enough to stay home alone. But I was lonely.

"When I was only a couple years older than you are now, a boy told me he liked me and wanted to be my boyfriend. We were together for a few months when, one day, I realized I was pregnant. I was so scared, because I was sure my dad was going to kill me. I hid it from him for as long as I could, but when it was impossible to hide any longer, I broke down and told him. We talked for weeks about what we would do. He told me he would do everything he could to support me."

Alex had turned slightly toward me and was listening intently. I cleared my throat and took a sip from the bottle of water I'd brought with me before I continued.

"I knew how I'd grown up. Never seeing my dad because he always worked. I was still in high school. I didn't have the skills to go and get a job that would support me and a baby. My dad had already busted his ass for ten years working two jobs just to support the both of us. What would happen if we added a baby to the mix? And I couldn't go to your biological father's family. He refused to acknowledge that you were his. And his family believed him over me. I knew that a baby needed clothes every couple months, diapers, formula, toys, and all the other array of things. I had no idea how I was going to be able to take care of you.

"I ran every scenario through my head. What happened if you got sick? We didn't have the money to pay for medical bills. It took me a long time to resign myself to the fact that there was no way I could give you the kind of life you deserved. And even though you were just this little thing growing inside my belly, I knew I had to do what I thought was best for you even if it broke my heart to do it. And I swear to you Alex, it shattered me. I couldn't think of myself though. So, I found a family I thought could give you all the things I knew I couldn't."

I breathed a small sigh of relief, having finally gotten that off my chest. I couldn't believe how freeing it was to finally let Alex know why I had done what I did. Even if he hated me, saying the words out loud, even now, I knew my choice back then had been the right one. I almost felt the heavy burden of guilt lighten off my shoulders. I would still always wonder what could have been, but I could now accept my choice no matter how difficult it was.

I tried to gauge his response to my story. He hadn't moved other than when he shifted toward me when I first started talking, so I wasn't sure how he took everything.

He studied me intently and didn't say anything for the longest time. Beads of sweat dripped down my back. The words he spoke just then made me jerk back in surprise. "Thank you. I may not have a perfect life, but I was loved and taken care of. I can't imagine being so young and having to make such a hard decision. I'm sure you did the best you could. So, yeah, thank you."

I burst into tears. The horrified look on Alex's face should have made me laugh, but it only made me cry harder. Warm arms wrapped around me and Connor pulled me close, and I buried my face into his hard chest and bawled. I could hear the confusion in Alex's voice as he asked, "What did I say? I'm so sorry. I didn't mean to make her cry."

"Just give her a minute," Connor told him. He cradled

my head against him as the tears continued. I wrapped my arms around his waist, and it was like I'd come home. I absorbed his strength and let out a shuddering breath as the final tears fell. Once I had myself under control, I wiped away the last of the tears.

I turned to Alex who looked like he was about to burst into tears. "You have no idea how happy I am to hear you say that. I was so afraid you were going to hate me. To hear you thank me threw me for a loop. I didn't expect that." I thought about the phone calls he'd made to me then. I needed to know what was going on.

"Alex," I tentatively began. "Why did you call me for help? I had no idea what was going on, and I was terrified when you hung up on me both times."

A number of emotions flashed across his face, fear being the most prevalent one. His gaze darted to Connor, apparently unsure of what to say. Connor cleared his throat before speaking. "It was a mistake. There is nothing you need to worry about."

The guilty expression on Alex's face said otherwise. I crossed my arms over my chest and glared at Connor. "Is that right?"

The stare-down between us was tense and Alex was shifting his weight back and forth in nervousness. Connor dropped his voice an octave and sent me his fierce Dom glare. "Yes, Bridget, that's right." I wouldn't be intimidated though. I was in mama bear mode at the moment.

"We'll talk about it later," I warned him.

"There's nothing to talk about Bridget. I said there was nothing to worry about, and there isn't. Now let it go." Alex sensed the determination behind Connor's words. He didn't seem to understand the tone even if I did, and he actually moved closer to me, apparently to protect me from Connor. For Alex's sake, I followed Connor's instructions and let it go. For now.

We spent the rest of the afternoon talking about Alex's hobbies and things he enjoyed. I told him about his grandfather and my shop. We got to know each other little by little. Finally, Alex said he needed to get back to the foster home where he'd been staying.

Hesitantly, I asked for a hug. He didn't move for a moment, then he wrapped his arms around me. When I hugged him back, he flinched in pain. I jerked back in surprise. I glanced over in question at Connor, but he just stared back at me, silent. I embraced him again, keeping my hands only lightly around him, and ran my hand down his head. I breathed in his smell and when we broke apart we both had tears in our eyes. He waved goodbye, and he and Connor left with an assurance from Connor that he would call me later.

I STARED at the three of them with hate-filled eyes. This was all *her* fault. I walked away, making plans to take care of business any way I had to.

CHAPTER 19

I DIDN'T TYPICALLY WORK on the weekends, but I was so far behind on my inventory that I needed to get caught up. I also figured it was a great way to keep my mind busy after meeting Alex today. Even Gina made mention of how neglectful I'd been with it lately. Between worry about Alex and my frustration with Connor, my focus was constantly elsewhere. I was glad I had great employees like Gina to pick up my slack. The customers loved her, and she had an eclectic sense of style that surprised most people, considering the borderline frumpy clothes she wore outside of Eden. For a woman in her mid-twenties, she more often than not dressed like someone's grandmother.

I worked at the boutique much later than I had planned, and it was dark by the time I finished my task and locked up. I didn't worry about walking home alone this late, even being this close to downtown. While we had the occasional break-in and car theft, there wasn't as much crime as you'd think for a town our size. I enjoyed the crisp, night air as I took in the smells of the city. I could faintly hear the thumping beat of music coming from the bar-lined street a few blocks away.

I thought about the college kids who were just starting their lives and had no worries beyond partying and having to get up early for a class. They had no idea about real life. It must be wonderful to be that free. Shaking off my melancholy, I opened the front door of my building and headed up the flights of stairs to my condo on the third floor. I could have taken the elevator, but I liked the exercise.

With my mind elsewhere, I didn't notice my front door was slightly ajar until I reached out to stick my key in the lock. I knew I'd closed it tightly and locked it before I left, so my senses were now on alert. I cautiously opened the door further and peeked my head in before stepping inside, not sure what to expect. I flipped the light switch next to the door, but the room remained dark. I attempted it again, but still nothing. Slowly my eyes adjusted to the darkness. As I warily walked inside and headed toward the kitchen to see if another light would work, I dug out my phone and dialed 9-1-1. All was quiet, but my hair stood on end. I couldn't tell if anything was out of place until I tripped over something and fell to my hands and knees with an oomph just as the operator answered. My phone skidded across the hardwood to the other side of the room.

"Shit," I muttered, as I picked myself up off the floor, my knees burning from the impact. No sooner had I stood and dusted myself off as I was grabbed from behind. A strong arm wrapped around my waist, trapping one of my arms against my side while the other covered my mouth to stifle my scream. The intruder hauled me up against his chest and dragged me toward the back of the condo where my bedroom was located. *Oh my God, was I about to be raped?*

I kicked and struggled, and using my free hand, I tried to pry his hand from my mouth to no avail. I couldn't get loose. Panic threatened to overwhelm me, but I forced myself to calm down and think. My dad made me take a self-defense course when I first moved into my place, and I tried to remember my training. I forced myself to go limp, suddenly making myself dead weight. With the unexpected move, he almost dropped me and had to readjust his handhold. I grabbed my chance.

In one fluid move, I tightened my body suddenly and jerked my head up, feeling a crunch when the back of my head made contact with his face.

"Fucking bitch, you broke my nose," rasped the nasally complaint behind me. My ears rang when the punch came to the side of my head. My vision blurred, and I shook my head to clear it. Before he had a chance to cover my mouth again, I drove my bony elbow into his gut and started screaming loud enough to bring the house down.

The man recovered from the jab I gave him and threw me to the ground. He dropped to his knee and started punching me, first in the face causing my head to snap to the side and my teeth to rattle. Blood filled my mouth. Punches continued to rain down on me, most hitting my ribs and kidneys, but occasionally he aimed for my face. On the verge of passing out from the pain, I heard the faint call of sirens in the background. Thank God.

As abruptly as the assault started, it stopped. I lay frozen on the floor, and out of the one eye that hadn't swollen shut, I saw the man run out the front door. I hissed in pain when I tried to move so I continued to lie there, helpless while I waited for someone to come to my rescue. I hadn't waited long when I heard footsteps racing down the hall. They stopped just outside the door and then the yelling came.

"Police! Is everything okay in there?" one of the disembodied voices outside my door asked. I almost laughed at the ludicrous question, but it hurt too much. Fuck no, everything wasn't okay in here. I groaned in agony, and a raspy, "I'm in here" came out. I cleared my throat and spoke louder. "I'm in here. I'm hurt pretty badly."

"Ma'am, are you alone?"

"Yes, he ran away right before you got here. Please, I think I need to go to the hospital." I winced when I tried moving again.

"We're coming in," the same voice warned. Two shadows crossed in front of my doorway, and I could tell that whoever it was had guns. I flinched and blinked when a flash of bright light shone down on my body. One of the cops rushed over to me while I heard the other calling for backup and EMS on his radio.

He dropped to his knees next to me. He started to reach out and touch me, but thought better of it. "Jesus, ma'am. The ambulance will be here soon. Do you know who did this?" he questioned.

I started to shake my head no, but every inch of my body hurt. "No, he was here when I got home. My door was open and when I walked in to investigate, he grabbed me after I tripped over something."

The second police officer called out, "There's an ottoman pushed out in the middle of the floor. It's the only thing that seems to have been disturbed."

The police officer next to me was young and cleared his throat before asking his next question. "Ma'am, I'm sorry to have to ask you this, but did he hurt you or touch you in any other way?" He looked extremely uncomfortable, shifting uneasily, and didn't make eye contact with me.

I knew what he meant, and I reassured him that I had not been sexually assaulted. The roar of more sirens came louder as additional emergency personnel arrived. Commotion sounded in the hall as the stretcher and paramedics exited the elevator and made their way into my place. The paramedics questioned me about my pain. They took vital signs and a cursory exam of my injuries before rolling me as gently as possible onto the stretcher. I couldn't help but cry out in pain with the movement. Just as they loaded me onto it, a familiar, but now grim, face came into my line of sight.

Daniel stopped directly in front of me. He reached out, pushed my hair back, and gently touched the left side of my face that had been spared most of the earlier punishment. He wiped away tears I had no idea were even falling. "Who the fuck did this to you, Bridget?"

"I don't know. There was someone in the house when I got home. He ran when the sirens got close." My head was pounding, and I didn't know how much longer I could take the pain.

As if reading my mind, the paramedics instructed everyone to move so they could get me to the hospital. I closed my eyes as they transported me out the door and into the waiting ambulance. I knew Daniel would follow and call Connor, so I kept my eyes closed and tried to ignore the pain. We hit a bump and the pain was so agonizing I couldn't take it, and I sank into oblivion.

CHAPTER 20

I WAS SITTING at the bar at Eden drinking my scotch as I waited for Bridget to arrive when my phone vibrated in my pocket. Phones weren't typically allowed in Eden, but ever since Alex had come into the picture, I kept it with me at all times in case he needed to reach me. When I saw who was calling, I was tempted to ignore it. I had no desire to talk to Webber, but then I thought about Alex and figured I better answer.

"It's Webber. We have a problem," he spoke before I could even say hello.

I sprang to attention with his words. "What?"

He clipped out the words. "Bridget's on her way to the hospital. Someone was in her apartment tonight and beat the shit out of her."

My ears buzzed, and I shook my head to clear the noise, not sure I'd heard him right. "Come again?" I asked.

He sighed in what sounded like disgust, but I heard the underlying worry in his tone. "We're headed to Pinegrove General. The guy really did a number on her. He used her

131

face as a punching bag, and if I had to guess she has, at minimum, severely bruised ribs. It's also possible she has a mild concussion. Anyway, I figured you needed to know."

I was already halfway to my car before he finished speaking. "I'm on my way. And Webber, thanks." I reluctantly told him.

I drove like a bat out of hell to the hospital. I needed to see with my own eyes that Bridget was okay. Fuck, this was all my fault. My instinct told me this was Malcolm's doing. Alex had repeatedly told me that Bridget was in danger, but I thought I could protect her. And with Alex temporarily out of Malcolm's reach, he must have set his sights on Bridget. I swerved into the hospital parking lot and had barely put the car in park before I'd jumped out and was sprinting to my woman.

I raced into the emergency department and spied Webber sprawled in one of the chairs at the back of the waiting room. I rushed over to him, needing to find out about Bridget. He must have heard my approach because he turned his head in my direction and sat up when I reached him.

"Where is she?" I snapped, impatient to see her and make sure she was okay.

"She's still in one of the exam rooms. They're stitching up the cut on both her cheek and above her eye. Then they're going to get an x-ray and CT scan to see about the ribs and concussion. That's all I can tell you." Webber replied, in a calm voice. I assumed he was trying to reassure me that she was going to be fine. I still needed to see her for myself.

Three excruciating hours later, a doctor entered the waiting room, and I leapt from my chair, ready to begin the interrogation. Webber had passed irritated about two hours ago. Every person wearing scrubs that came through the door received the third degree about Bridget whether they knew anything or not. After I interrogated the fourth nurse, Webber gave up trying to stop me. He'd fallen asleep an hour ago.

"How's Bridget Carter doing? They brought her in about three hours ago."

"Are you Connor Black?"

"Yes, now tell me how she is."

"Ms. Carter is in stable condition. She has been asking for you and knew you would be waiting to hear how she was. Her x-rays came back negative for cracked ribs, but they are bruised, and the CT scan showed no skull fracture, but she does have a minor concussion. She'll need to be on bed rest for another day and she'll have a whopper of a headache for a few more days with the possibility of some dizziness and double vision. She won't be able to drive for at least a week or until she follows up with her primary care physician. Overall, she is an extremely lucky woman. She was severely beaten, and it definitely could have been worse. Does she live with anyone or is there someone she can stay with for a few days?"

Without any hesitation and before thinking it all the way through I said, "Bridget will be staying with me. Now, can I please see her?"

With a nod, he led me through the doors, past exam rooms and curtained off areas and stopped before a slightly opened door. He indicated for me to enter. I lightly knocked, slowly opened the door, and,careful to not wake her if she'd fallen asleep. I spied her lying on the gurney, eyes closed, and bruises on the entire right side of her face, which only highlighted the stitches in her cheek and above her eye. Fury raged through me, and I had to quash the urge to punch a hole in the wall.

"I didn't mean to wake you."

She blinked a couple times before her gaze focused in on me. She attempted to smile, but winced in pain and reached up to touch her face to assess her injury. Bridget groaned in pain when she tried to shift positions.

"You didn't wake me. I was just resting. And trying not to move. Fuck, my whole body feels like I've been run over by a train. My head is killing me, too."

Even with the bruises marring her face, Bridget was still the most beautiful woman I'd ever seen. I intended to do everything I could to find the bastard who did this and fuck up his entire existence. No one hurt my woman. And yes, she was my woman. When I got that phone call from Webber telling me Bridget had been injured, my heart stopped. I was madly in love with this woman and I needed to stop pushing her away. Like she once said, she needed a man with the balls to go after what he wanted. It was time for me to grow a pair and fight for her. Even if it was my inner demons I had to fight.

Bridget was unlike any woman I'd ever known. I had to have faith that she wouldn't reject me based on my superficial looks, unlike other women. I still needed to keep that other side of me, the darker side, reined in, but I needed to claim this woman before someone else did. The question was, was I strong enough? Looking at her lying there, I knew I had to be.

"I'm sorry you're hurting, baby. Where the hell is the nurse with some pain medicine?"

"Connor, it's fine. I took something not that long ago. It just needs to kick in. I'll be all right in a little bit. Really."

I could sense she was puzzling something out inside that gorgeous head of hers when she barely cocked her head and narrowed her eyes at me.

"Did you just call me 'baby'?"

Oddly, heat rose to my cheeks. I don't know that I'd ever blushed before in my life. I had to clear my throat before answering. "Is there a problem with me calling you baby?"

She hesitated only briefly, but enough to make my heart stop. "Not necessarily, but I'm a little confused. You've pushed me away more than once, and now you're calling me pet names. The mixed signals you've been sending are enough to drive a person to drink. I'm not sure what your angle is."

I reached out to clasp her hand in mine. "There is no angle. I could have lost you tonight, and it made me realize how short life is and that we don't always get second chances. I want a second chance. I care about you, Bridget. I don't know where this could lead, but I'm ready to find out. No more pushing you away. It ends now, especially because I know you want me too. I'm done fucking around. It's time to claim what's mine."

"Yours, huh? Just like that, you're going to claim me like I'm a piece of property? You seem awfully sure of yourself."

She was toeing the line of bratty with her words, and it was time to put her in check. "Damn right you're mine, Bridget. You and I both know it. Now, stop arguing with me. Just know we'll be discussing how things are going to be between us soon. Understand?"

She nodded slowly. "Yes, Sir."

"Good girl." She almost purred at the praise. "You'll be staying with me until I find out who did this to you." Her mouth opened, about to argue. "This is not up for discussion, Bridget. You *will* stay with me. I need to be able to protect you. I refuse to lose you. Once you're discharged, we'll stop by your place so you can pick up things you might need. Then, for the duration, you'll be with me. Now, get some sleep. I need to talk to Webber, but I'll be here when you wake up."

Even through her yawn she fought me. "You're awfully bossy, even for a Dom. But I'll sleep because I'm tired."

I had to stifle a smile, because I secretly enjoyed her bratty side on occasion. It would give me an excuse to warm up that ass. She kept me on my toes and was never predictable. I would never be bored with her around. Our living arrangement was going to take some getting used to, but I was looking forward to keeping Bridget in line. My hand tingled in anticipation of all the spankings I knew she was going to earn. I watched as her heavy-lidded eyes finally closed and a soft sigh escaped her lips. I knew she was out for the count. I quietly left the room and headed out to where I figured Webber still waited.

CHAPTER 21

THE FIRST THING I noticed upon waking was that everything hurt. I wasn't in total agony anymore, but shit still hurt. I opened my eyes and blinked, trying to bring the tiled ceiling into focus. I lay there for a minute gathering my bearings. Then I remembered where I was and what had happened. I didn't know how long I'd been asleep, but if the pain I was in was any indication, it hadn't been long enough. Damn, I hated hospitals. The last time I had been here was when I'd given birth to Alex. Based on how I currently felt, I had a feeling I wasn't going anywhere any time soon. Damn.

"Hey beautiful."

I slowly turned my head, wincing slightly, and spotted Connor sitting in the darkened corner. I drank in the sight of him looking cramped and uncomfortable in the too small chair. He was wearing the same clothes he'd been in when he was here before, and he had a crease in his cheek where it looked like he'd been sleeping on it. Even still, he was the most handsome man I'd ever met.

"How long have I been asleep?" I asked, groggily, my voice scratchy.

Connor moved the chair closer to the bed and reached for my hand. I'm not sure if he was trying to comfort me or himself. "About ten hours. It's 4:00 in the afternoon now. You needed the sleep so I didn't want to disturb you. Are you feeling any better?"

I took inventory of my aches and pains and realized that, while sore, I wasn't in the agonizing pain I'd been in when I first arrived at the hospital or even when Connor first came in.

"Let's just say I won't be doing any jumping jacks anytime soon." I laughed. "But, seriously, I don't feel like crying anymore, so I'll take it. I have a small headache and my side hurts, but I could be dead so I guess in the grand scheme of things, that's not so bad."

Fury unlike any I'd ever seen before flashed across Connor's face. "I'll kill whoever did this to you, Bridget. I promise you."

Shock had me immobilized. I could see by the look on his face that he was entirely serious. I was both horrified and yet strangely filled with awe that someone would go to such extreme lengths for me. I wasn't even sure how to respond. I was saved from saying anything by a knock on the door. A young nurse poked her head in.

"Oh," she smiled brightly, "you're awake. I hate to bother you, but there is a detective here who would like to speak with you, Ms. Carter."

I exchanged a glance with Connor and hoped he behaved himself.

"Please show him in."

She opened the door wider and, with a wave of her hand,

ushered Daniel in. He looked a little haggard, like sleep eluded him. He was still an extremely good-looking man, but my body didn't come alive like it did with Connor.

"Bridget. Black." He inclined his head. "I needed to ask you some questions about what happened last night. I might have a lead from an eyewitness who saw someone run out of the building about the same time as your assault, but I still want to hear what went down in your words."

He pulled out his notepad and pen that always seemed to be with him. "What time did you arrive home last night?"

"I can't remember the exact time, but I finished up at the store around 8:30. I took my time walking home so I probably got there around 9:00."

He scribbled in his notebook. "And what happened when you got to your house?"

I told my story, and Daniel took numerous notes. Connor cursed occasionally in the background, but I kept my eyes on Daniel, not wanting to see the expression on Connor's face. A churning began in my belly as nausea hit me when I remembered the terror I felt not knowing if I was about to be raped. I took deep calming breaths, trying not to have a panic attack.

"He ran out of the house, and the two officers arrived shortly afterward. You know what happened after that."

Daniel had briefly stopped writing in his notebook during my retelling, especially when I got to the part where the intruder had been carrying me back to my room. Out of the corner of my eye, I noticed Connor's fists clenching and unclenching.

"Do you remember seeing anything or noticing anything about the intruder? Any fragrances like cologne? Could you tell how tall he was? What about his voice? Did he say anything? Don't think any detail is too small."

I didn't want to remember what had happened or what could have happened. I just wanted it all to go away. But I knew that wouldn't help anyone, so I thought back to last night and tried to remember any possible detail. "I didn't notice any special smells, and I can only tell you he was taller than me, but not by much I don't think. He didn't say anything until I head-butted him and possibly broke his nose. He started swearing. Other than that, there's nothing I can remember. I was too focused on not puking from the pain that I didn't pay attention as he ran out the door. I'm sorry I can't be more helpful."

Daniel put his notebook and rose. "You've been very helpful. I'm going to follow up on the possible lead and see if it goes anywhere. I'd like to talk with you more a little later. Can I stop by your house in a few days and speak with you?"

Before I could even speak, Connor butted in. "She won't be returning home any time soon."

"Oh, and where will she be?"

"With me."

My gaze bounced back and forth between the two men who continued to stare each other down. It was almost comical to watch the non-verbal communication between the two. Connor's chest was puffed out and his arms were crossed over it. As though something specific passed between the men, Daniel's expression changed slightly. He broke eye contact with Connor, and if I hadn't been looking at him I would have missed the small nod. He then turned back to look at me.

"Well then, I know where I can reach you when I need to

speak with you next. I'll be in touch sometime in the next few days."

He moved to the door and opened it to leave. He paused, and turned his head toward me again before speaking softly. "I'm really glad you're safe, Bridget."

Before I could thank him, he quickly walked out the door, closing it behind him, leaving me feeling like I'd just lost a friend.

CHAPTER 22

I LEARNED something about Bridget at the hospital. She was a terrible patient, and had no idea how to lie still. She was constantly getting up and moving even though the doctor told her she needed to rest. I understood that moving around a little was good for her, but she was always in motion. She suffered from occasional dizziness due to the concussion and needed to take a quick break from what she was doing until it went away. Other than that, she didn't stop. She was constantly walking around the room, flashes of her ass driving me insane.

They kept Bridget overnight Sunday for observation, and early Monday morning, she was released from the hospital. We had picked up a few things from her house that she needed and then I got her settled in at my place. Gina had taken over running the store while Bridget was recovering. And even though it probably wasn't my place, I told Gina that she would remain in charge for a few more days. I planned on making sure Bridget stayed off her feet for a while until she recovered. Plus, the fact that she was finally in my house and my bed was something I didn't want to change any time soon. I planned on keeping her here as long as I could. Forever, if possible. She just didn't know it yet.

I didn't know how long I could resist her now that she was finally in my grasp. Seeing her day in and day out was going to drive me mad. I wanted to touch her all the time. To reassure myself that she was really here. I had no idea how I was going to sleep next to her tonight and not reach out for her.

I showed her around the house when we first got there, and I caught her wincing once because of the bruised ribs when she turned a certain way. It was then that a fury unlike any I'd felt before came over me. Instinct was pointing a finger at Malcolm Shipman.

For the last few days, my entire focus had been on Bridget. But now I needed to get back to the reason why she came to me in the first place—to help Alex. Knowing she was safe with me, I could relax a little and shift my attention to Alex and getting him out of the hands of that bastard.

"I need to leave for a few hours. Are you going to behave yourself and rest while I'm gone?"

"Of course. What kind of trouble do you expect me to get into?"

"With you, I have no idea. But I need you to stay put and get some rest. We still don't know who did this to you, Bridget. And until he's caught, I want to know you're safe. Which means you stay here and behave."

Bridget's playfulness faded a little with my words. "I understand, Sir. I'll be a good sub and follow your orders. Today."

I could only shake my head. I knew I had my hands full with this one. But I wouldn't have it any other way. I fucking loved this woman, brattiness and all. I was going to enjoy attempting to tame her. I certainly didn't want to change anything about her, but I loved having some fun and pushing her to her limits. Which was something we needed to discuss. It was time to begin more fully communicating with each other. We certainly had not been practicing safe BDSM. And I took full responsibility for that.

She had been correct when she said she didn't know what was expected of her. And that was no way to treat a sub, especially my sub. Subs needed rules and boundaries. They want to please their Dom, but they can't do that if they've not been given the tools to do it. Without that foundation, resentment would be the result. I felt I had failed my responsibility as a Dom to guide her and direct her. That was about to change.

"Before I leave, though, there are some things we need to discuss."

She made a face. "Well, that sounds ominous."

"Not really. Come here."

When she was within arm's length, I pulled her against me so she rested in the cradle of my hips. Unconsciously, she leaned into me and wrapped her arms around the back of my neck.

"We need to talk limits. It's my fault we've been remiss in this. But I'm trying to be more open and communicate enough to meet your needs. So, this is me communicating. You are now in my home. The rules are much different here than they are at your house. Here, I am Master of all things. I am the one in control. I'm not expecting you to be my slave. I have a housekeeper who cleans, and we can share meal prep. I don't expect you to wait on me hand and foot. However, when we are in the bedroom, you belong to me. I need to know what your soft and hard limits are. Are you on birth control, because I want to feel you skin to skin? Do you have any triggers? Most importantly, what is your safe word?"

My spine tingled and my cock became semi-hard as she played with my hair. I didn't realize my head was such an erogenous zone. Not many women had the opportunity to touch me like this. I was realizing how much I enjoyed it.

"Well, Sir, I only have a few hard limits. I'm not into blood, golden showers, or scat. I don't do needles or knives. I'm also not into age play. I don't have any triggers that I've discovered in any of my play. I'm on the pill. so I'm okay with forgoing condoms. Also, my safe word is *unicorn*."

"Unicorn?" I couldn't help but smirk a little at this.

She pulled my hair. "What's wrong with unicorn?"

I could only shake my head. "Nothing. Nothing at all. Now that we have that out of the way, if I have special instructions for you during the day, I will make sure you know exactly what they are so there are no misunderstandings. I have one very specific rule in the bedroom and that is you do not touch me unless I tell you to. This is non-negotiable. Do you have any questions?"

I sensed her evaluating everything I'd told her. I could almost see the wheels turning in her gorgeous head.

"No questions, Sir. But, may I speak freely?"

I nodded my assent.

"How long will this rule be in effect? You obviously have a reason for it, and as my Sir, you don't have to explain to me, because it's your rule. But, trust goes both ways, Connor. I've trusted you with everything from the very beginning. Besides my father, you were the first person who ever knew about Alex.

"Do you know how hard it was for me to open up to you about giving up my child? It's a secret that has tortured me for years. I was ashamed of my choices. So I understand how difficult it is to open yourself up to hurt. To show vulnerability. I've been there. But there comes a time when you have to take that leap. You have to reciprocate that trust. I swear to you, Sir, you can trust me with whatever it is you're hiding."

She leaned up and softly brushed her lips across mine. It wasn't enough. I needed to taste her sweetness. I deepened the kiss, teasing her lips with my tongue, coaxing them open. I loved her flavor and would never get enough of it. I needed to put a stop to this before it was too late. She was still too sore. Reluctantly, I pulled away.

"Thank you for your trust, Bridget. I am thankful for it. And I do trust you. Old habits are hard to break. I'll take what you've said into consideration. Trusting people hasn't worked out well for me in the past. Just be patient with me. Now, I need to get going. Remember what I said, Bridget. Rest."

I left the house before I changed my mind about taking her to bed. The first place I needed to stop was my office. Then I needed to pay a visit to a couple of people, including Malcolm Shipman.

CHAPTER 23

AFTER STOPPING at my office and gathering all the research I'd done on the Shipmans, I headed to the precinct to hopefully catch Webber in his office. The officer at the desk said he should be back shortly so I paced the lobby as I waited for him to arrive. After twenty minutes, I spotted him coming around the corner. When he saw me, he just waved at me and indicated that I follow him. He led me back to the same office where we first spoke about Alex.

"Have a seat, Black. How's Bridget?"

"She's settling in. Still recovering, but doing well. How was that lead you thought you had?"

Webber leaned back in his chair, propped his feet up on his desk, and crossed his arms behind his head. A sense of déjà vu washed over me.

"You know I'm not at liberty to share that information with you. This is an ongoing police investigation, and well, you're not the police. Now, since I know that's not all you came here to talk to me about, what can I do for you?"

"You're right. That's not all I came here to discuss. I

wanted to show you something. You know, in case you hadn't figured it out yourself. Tell me what you think of this." I opened the folder I'd brought with me and slid the first set of papers across the desk. Webber shifted from his reclined position and began skimming over the information. As much as I hated to admit it, Webber was smart. I knew he'd draw the same conclusion I had. I just needed to give him time.

After a few minutes, he looked up at me. "Fuck. How long have you been hanging on to this? And how did you get this information? Never mind, I don't want to know. This sure is some interesting stuff you dug up. It appears our neighborhood child abuser has now leapt to potential murder suspect. You're killing me here, Black. You know that, right?"

"There are inconsistencies about the car accident. I just happened to stumble upon a report that shows that the brake lines had been cut and foul play was suspected. Yet, somehow that report got buried, and the official report says they were hit by a drunk driver. How do you explain that?"

"Someone doctored the report."

I was glad Webber and I were on the same page. "What reason would someone have to doctor an official police report? My guess is money. Someone was paid a lot of money to make a homicide look like an accident. You and I both know it makes sense, Webber. The Shipmans each had a million dollars in life insurance with Alex designated as their beneficiary. Malcolm Shipman kindly steps up as guardian and is named trustee of the account for Alex's inheritance. The man works in retail for fuck's sake. He has a modest—and I mean modest—personal savings account. Yet he drives a $90,000 car. Which he paid cash for. There are also some significant withdrawals. I did a little more digging, and it seems our friend Malcolm has a slight gambling problem. Did you know that the Shipmans had also taken out a life insurance policy on Alex?"

Webber sighed as he returned to his reclined position. "Let me guess. It's for another million bucks?"

"Ding, ding, ding. We have a winner. Obviously nothing can happen to Alex this soon after his parents' deaths because that would certainly raise some serious red flags. But, if my suspicions are correct, then it's only a matter of time before Malcolm Shipman becomes not only the grieving brother, but the grieving uncle."

I LEFT the station and made another stop. I needed to check on Alex. He was still in the foster home, but after my conversation with Webber, it looked like that wouldn't last much longer. Alex had been right in that nobody was going to find any evidence of abuse. Our time was running out, because Alex would be returning to his uncle's house soon. Webber was going to do what he could on his end to find out who might have falsified the accident report and to look into Malcolm's gambling habits and who he might owe money to.

I pulled up to the house where Alex was staying and idled for a few minutes as I thought about what I was going to say to him. He was old enough to know the truth, but I didn't know if now was the right time to tell him. I wanted to protect him from the ugliness, but he needed to know what he was up against when he returned to Malcolm's. I jogged up the walk and knocked on the front door. I heard a dog barking in the background and then some yelling for the dog to shut up.

When the front door opened, a sloppily dressed man stood there, a beer in one hand and a cigarette in the other. "Can I help you?"

Biting back a scathing response, I took a deep breath to try and calm myself. "I'm here to see Alex."

The guy turned and yelled over his shoulder. "Alex, you got company."

Footsteps raced down the stairs and Alex quickly appeared at the bottom of them. His entire body relaxed when he saw me.

"Hi, Connor."

"Hey, kid. I was hoping we could talk for a bit." I turned to the person I assumed, was Alex's foster parent. "My name is Connor Black. I own Blacklight Securities. Here's my card as well as the number where you can reach Detective Daniel Webber. I'd like to spend a few minutes speaking with Alex, if you don't mind."

The man looked me up and down and walked away without a word. Jesus, I really needed to talk to Webber about the choices in foster parents around here. There was something fucked about the system, because it certainly didn't seem to have improved since I was in the foster system. I blew off the guy, and Alex and I left the house. We walked side by side down the sidewalk. I didn't have a destination in mind, I just wanted time alone with him.

"So, what's wrong?"

Damn, the kid didn't beat around the bush. Another trait he got from his mother.

"I spoke to my friend, Daniel, today. You remember him, right?" When he nodded, I continued. "Well, anyway, I wanted to ask you a couple questions about your uncle. Don't feel bad if you can't answer them. I just wanted to speak to you first. Have you ever heard your uncle talking about owing money to anyone? Maybe on the phone some time?"

We continued walking as he thought about it. "Well, there was this one time when I heard him arguing with someone about getting their money to them. But I must have made some type of noise, because he was suddenly quiet. Then he told whoever he was talking to that he was taking care of it, and he hung up the phone. Now that I think about it, he caught me trying to eavesdrop and slapped me for it."

"Is that the only thing you can think of? It's pretty important, Alex."

"Yeah, that's the only time I remember it coming up. Why? What's going on, Connor?"

We had reached the neighborhood park, and I headed over to a bench.

"When I first found you for Bridget, I needed to know what I was up against since, both times you called her, you indicated you were in some kind of trouble. I needed to find out everything I could about you, your uncle, and your parents. I wanted to make sure you were safe. I have a friend who is really good with computers. She found out some stuff that even the police wouldn't have been able to find."

I stopped, trying to find the right words to explain to a thirteen-year-old-boy that, more than likely, his uncle had murdered his parents. It was a total shit storm, and there really wasn't an easy way to say it. Alex waited patiently for me to finish explaining.

"There appears to be an incorrect report about how your parents died. There's no real easy way to say this, but I don't think the accident was really an accident. There was evidence that shows their brake lines were cut."

Alex sat stone-faced and silent.

"Your parents had significant life insurance policies, both for themselves and for you. With you listed as their beneficiary, but being a minor, the money was put into a trust. My friend was able to take a look at the trust, and it seems as if there is quite a bit missing. And we think we know who's taking it."

"It's highly likely, yes."

Alex turned his head to look me straight in the eye. "And you're also saying that he probably killed them, aren't you?"

I hated that I was the one doing this. I wanted to be anywhere but here. "We don't have proof of anything right now. Webber is looking into some things."

"My case worker came by earlier today. She said I'll be returning to my uncle's house in the next couple of days. I'm afraid, Connor. He's going to kill me too, isn't he?"

CHAPTER 24

FOUR DAYS HAD PASSED since my meetings with Webber and Alex and a week since the attack on Bridget. I hadn't known what to say to Alex other than to reassure him that I would do everything in my power to protect him. I hated this feeling of helplessness. It brought back too many memories. And even though I was trying to overcome my insecurities, not only for myself, but for Bridget, I couldn't change overnight. We slept in the same bed every night, and while we had done a lot of touching and petting, I had forced myself to stop before things went further. However, she had been complaining less and less of any pain in her ribs.

Webber had called me earlier while I was at the office to let me know that Alex would be returning to Malcolm's home in the morning. After I'd hung up with him, I thought it might be a good idea to pay a little visit to Malcolm. I wasn't going to kick the shit out of him, no matter how tempted I might be, but perhaps putting the fear of god into him might make me feel better. It was almost time for him to get home from work. I'd just head over to the house before returning home to my woman.

I arrived shortly after 6:00 pm, knocked on the door, and waited until I heard a faint "Just a minute" come from inside the house. I waited impatiently, until finally the door opened.

"Yes, can I help you?"

Immediately, I noticed the tape across his nose. Bridget had said she thought she broke the intruder's nose. My gut had said Malcolm had something to do with it. This confirmed it in my opinion. It was too coincidental. Now that I was face to face with the piece of shit, I wanted to kill him. It took every ounce of willpower I had to stop myself from reaching out and beating him to death.

"You don't recognize me, do you?"

He looked quizzically at me for a few minutes before shaking his head. "Should I?"

"My name is Connor. I met you at the gym a couple of weeks ago. I asked you to spot me during my workout."

"Oh, yeah, I remember now. What are you doing here? How did you know where I lived?" I could hear the puzzlement in his voice.

"I know a lot about you Malcolm. A lot. In fact, I probably know more about you than you would want me to. Like the fact that there's a certain bookie in town you owe a substantial amount of money to. I know you like to hit people who can't defend themselves. I even know about the prostitute you picked up a few years ago. Peaches was her street name, I believe."

He stared at me in shock. And fear. Bullies only got off on tormenting those smaller than them. "What do you want?"

"First off, you're going to keep your fucking hands off

Alex. Second, you're going to allow Bridget visitation. Oh, and if you are ever within ten feet of her, I won't hesitate to beat the everloving shit out of you."

I stepped into his personal space and leaned forward until our faces almost touched. "And just so you know, if you lay a single finger on either Alex or Bridget again, I will kill you. Slowly. Painfully. And no one will ever find your body when I'm through with it. You don't fucking touch what is mine. They're both my family. And I protect my family. I'll be watching you."

I walked away before I did something I would regret.

I DIDN'T WANT to go home with this much anger coursing through me, so I drove around for thirty minutes before my blood stopped boiling. Seeing that bandage on Malcolm's nose had me on the verge of spontaneous combustion. I kept picturing the description she gave of the man dragging her toward her room. I wouldn't have put it past Malcolm to rape her in addition to beating the shit out of her. He was the type of guy who got off on making others feel powerless. That's the way it was with bullies. It wasn't healthy for me that the scene kept playing over and over. I needed something to replace it. And I knew exactly what that something was.

I clicked the Bluetooth and spoke into the microphone. "Call Bridget."

As I waiting for the call to connect, I replaced the images in my head with other images. Better images. My cock hardened, and I couldn't wait to get home.

"Hello," Bridget answered.

"Hello, my gorgeous sub. Have you been a good girl while I've been gone?"

"Yes, Sir."

"I'm glad to hear that. I should be home shortly. Have you eaten yet?"

"No, Sir, I was waiting for you."

"Don't wait for me. I want you to eat before I get home, because I have a task for you."

"But what about you, Sir? You need to eat as well."

"Thank you for thinking of me, but I'll pick up something on the way. I'll be home in about an hour. Once you've eaten, here's what you will do for me."

I went on to explain exactly what I wanted from her. I disconnected the phone once I'd given her my instructions and smiled at the thought of what tonight held.

CHAPTER 25

I POSITIONED myself on the bed on all fours as Connor had requested. I expected him home any time now, and I wanted to make sure I was ready when he arrived. I was nervous about what would happen tonight, because I planned on giving him a little push, and I didn't know how he was going to respond. I enjoyed the touching and kissing we'd been doing, but I needed more. I knew he'd been holding back for a variety of reasons, not the least that he was afraid of hurting me. But my ribs had been feeling better for a couple of days. I wasn't completely pain-free, but at least now it was tolerable.

Everything was seemingly perfect in our relationship except for this one thing. I could sense that he was desperate to trust me, but he just didn't quite know how to take that leap. I hated pushing the issue, but I didn't know how much longer I was going to be able to live this way. Even after only a few days, I knew something needed to give. Eventually, I was going to become resentful that he was refusing to share all of himself with me. I only prayed I didn't cause him to pull away from me.

"Well, well, well. If that isn't a lovely sight to behold." I had been so wrapped up in my musings, I hadn't even heard Connor enter the bedroom. I turned my head and tossed my hair so I could peek at him over my shoulder. I gave my ass a little shake. There was no way that after his specific instructions that he would be satisfied with only the barest of touching tonight. I planned on doing everything in my power to make sure that he finished what he started.

"I never heard you come in, Sir. I hope this is to your liking."

A soft caress along the back of my thigh and up my spine sent a shiver of arousal through me. Connor leaned down to press a welcoming kiss to my mouth.

"This is definitely to my liking. Your pussy and ass are on perfect display, just begging for attention. Especially that ass. I've been extremely neglectful in my attention to these two gorgeous globes and what's hidden in between them."

With his words, he trailed his fingers along the crease of my thigh and skimmed up and down my crack. It was a tease for what I hoped was about to come. I loved anal sex. The nerve endings that were stimulated during anal caused a spark to explode inside me. It was a feeling unlike any other, and I craved it. Connor moved his fingers lower and dipped one inside my pussy. He coated the digit in my cream before blazing a path upward where he began circling my asshole. He started with a gentle touch, not quite entering, but tracing round and round, stimulating the puckered hole that opened in anticipation of being filled by his cock.

I couldn't help but clench slightly as the finger finally entered me. In and out Connor pressed, going farther each time. When I relaxed my muscles and tried to push back, a sharp crack sounded and heat spread across my ass cheek.

"Don't move."

Coldness spread down my crack and across my anus as I realized Connor was dribbling lube on me. He must have grabbed some while I was still unaware he'd entered the house. He withdrew his finger and spread the wetness around, coating every inch of my hole before pushing it back in to spread it around inside. More lube was poured and then a small stretch followed and I knew he'd added another finger. I forced my body to remain still as he thrust his fingers in and out of me. His thrusts quickened, and I bit my lip as a moan of ecstasy escaped. All my nerve endings were firing, and all I wanted to do was move.

I could feel my body tightening in preparation for a glorious climax when Connor suddenly removed his fingers. I had to hold back the groan of disappointment. I heard rustling behind me, but I remained still. I didn't want to do anything to distract Connor from his task and remind him that I'd only recently been injured. It didn't matter that I was feeling much better. If he thought he was hurting me in any way, he would stop what he was doing immediately. I refused to allow that to happen. I missed feeling him inside me.

The bed dipped and warmth surrounded me as Connor cradled my hips in his, his leg hair tickling the back of my thighs. He gently pushed forward, his cock positioned in my crack where it slid up and down with each forward thrust of his hips. His upper body was bent over mine and he was flush against my back. I couldn't stop the slight flinch and sigh of disappointment as the fabric of his shirt separated our flesh. Connor stopped moving at the sound.

He lowered his head, and I felt petal soft kisses across my shoulder. I was continuously surprised by how gentle he could be. It was a contradiction to the power he housed in his body. It often seemed he was holding back, restraining his body's urgings to plunder and ravage.

"Your skin is like silk, soft and supple. Your body deserves to be worshipped and treated with the utmost care."

He'd placed his hands next to mine on the bed when he leaned over me. He moved them until they were on top and he laced our fingers. He didn't move; it was though he wanted to savor our physical bond. He nuzzled my hair and inhaled deeply, breathing in my scent.

Briefly, Connor untwined our right hands. I felt him reach behind me to grasp his cock and with excruciating slowness, he pressed it against my puckered hole. He began a gentle thrusting motion, pushing his cock farther and farther into my ass. I relaxed my muscles as best I could to help ease him inside. Inch by inch he entered me, until, finally, his hips were flush against mine.

He locked our hands together again and remained motionless while I adjusted to the fit. No more words were spoken as Connor tightened his grip on my hands and initiated again the gentle in and out motion. He kept a slow pace, torturing me with my need for him to go faster. But Connor wasn't having any of it. This was his show, and he was the one in control.

He reached up with his left hand to cup my breast, lightly tweaking the nipple. His fingers then trailed down my stomach until he reached my mound. He cupped my sex in his large hand and curled his fingers until they pressed against my pussy. He didn't enter me, just rubbed the tips up and down my slit, causing more cream to drip down my thighs. He adjusted positions so he hit a new spot inside my ass as he began circling my clit. The dual sensations had me panting in arousal.

I could feel his heartbeat against my back through his shirt, and soon, mine matched his rhythm. Our connection was visceral. My climax continued to build with each thrust of his cock and with each flick against my clit until I couldn't control my release. It exploded out of me. Connor groaned behind me as he peaked immediately after I did. I felt his seed fill my ass. I collapsed in exhaustion. Connor slowly pulled out of me and rose from the bed. I continued to lie there as I heard him enter the bathroom and turn on the water. He returned and bathed me with a warm cloth as I replayed our encounter. Physically, he'd satisfied my needs. Emotionally, I was bereft. I needed to make him understand what I needed from him as my Dom.

CHAPTER 26

INSTINCTIVELY KNOWING it was now or never, I flipped over and moved up on my knees, ignoring the twinge in my ass. I had a feeling this was my only chance to get through to Connor.

"I wish you would stop hiding from me. I'm here, and I'm not going anywhere, Connor." I cupped his face and stared into his eyes, hoping my sincerity and the depth of my feelings shone through. An eternity passed where neither of us moved. I truly thought we had built more trust between us, but apparently, I guessed wrong. I sighed in defeat and removed my hands. I sat back on my heels in the now awkward silence. When I couldn't take it anymore, I laid back down, my back to Connor. Tears burned behind my closed eyes.

I don't know how much time passed when a gravelly cough sounded behind me. "My dad died when I was five. He hadn't been feeling well for a few days so he laid down to take a nap while my mom and I went to the grocery store.

He was dead when we got home. The doctors said he'd had a massive heart attack."

I started to turn, but Connor stopped me. "Stay there. I need you to just lie there, please. Otherwise, I'll never get through this."

I heard the pain behind his words, and it broke my heart. This beautiful, strong man had been broken at one point, and I wanted to kill the person who hurt him, because it was obvious someone had. I couldn't imagine the struggle it was for him to splay himself open to me. I knew he kept things bottled up, but I never would have imagined what he would tell me next.

"My mom remarried within a year. She had never been alone before, and I don't think she knew how to cope with that. The guy she married was all right. I never called him my stepdad, because he was no kind of dad to me. He pretty much ignored me, until he was injured at work one day when I was eight. He got hooked on alcohol and pills to numb his pain. Unfortunately, for my mom and me, he was a mean drunk. Nothing either of us did was right. It started with a slap one time. Of course, he was penitent and begged my mom for forgiveness. But then it happened again. And again. Only each time, it escalated.

"I had recently turned thirteen when everything came to a head. I finally found the courage to fight back. But it was no use. I was too weak and small, and my mother's husband was so far gone nothing could have stopped him. It was like he'd been possessed by the devil himself. In his rage, he dumped a pot of boiling water on me, giving me second and third degree burns over a quarter of my body, the majority of it focused on my back. I blacked out from the pain. When I came to, the paramedics and police were there and my mother was dead. He'd stabbed her to death with a kitchen knife. He was sent to prison, and I bounced around from foster home to foster home until I turned eighteen."

I didn't bother to stop the flow of tears cascading down my cheeks. I held my breath as I turned back toward him, hoping he wouldn't stop me. I needed to comfort him, and perhaps myself, because I had a feeling he'd received very little comfort in his life. When I finally faced him, he sat stone-faced looking neither left nor right. There were tension lines around his mouth, and his fists were clenched at his sides.

Hesitantly, I reached out and clasped his hand in mind. I slowly sat up and enfolded him in my loving embrace. I didn't say anything, not wanting him to run scared. I held him in my arms until he slowly began to relax. Finally, I couldn't hold back any longer.

"I'm so sorry, Connor. You know none of that is your fault, right? I mean, you were just a child. There was no way you could have stopped him. And I'm so sorry you've been holding the pain in for so long. Thank you for trusting me. It means more to me than you know."

CHAPTER 27

I PULLED AWAY SLIGHTLY, forcing her to loosen her arms, and I couldn't quite look her in the eye. Telling her what had happened to me was only the tip of the iceberg. Actually showing her scared the shit out of me and required more trust than I'd ever shown anyone. I inhaled deeply, trying to breathe in the control I needed to keep going with my confession. Now came the true test of Bridget's feelings. With trembling hands, I slowly began to unbutton my shirt. Her eyes followed the movement as more of my chest became bared to her regard.

I kept my gaze on her face, anticipating the moment she would turn away. Finally, my shirt was entirely unbuttoned and I peeled it back and down my arms, fully exposing my front to her. Tears that had only recently dried, welled in her eyes and threatened to fall. I watched as she blinked them back. Bridget's eyes darted up to mine, and I refused to look away. Maintaining eye contact with me, she hesitantly reached out and laid her hand on my chest, right over my heart.

Her stare dropped back to my chest as she began tentatively tracing the scars that decorated it. Each one burned, but none more so than the ones on my back. Before I could guess her intent, Bridget leaned forward and laid the softest of kisses directly on the largest scar. It was as if a butterfly was dancing across my skin. It tingled and sizzled, and a different kind of burn developed. She dropped kiss after kiss, each one a little longer. I even felt the flick of her tongue and a shudder of arousal flowed through me.

Bridget's hands never left my body, and her eyes stayed locked on mine as she scooted next to me. She then moved slowly off the bed, and I lost sight of her as she stood behind me. A sharp gasp was the only sound in the room as she finally looked her fill of my mangled back. I tensed as I visualized exactly what she was seeing. The mottled skin varying from shades of pink to shades of brown. The shiny, puckered skin in some spots and the long, ropey, thickened strands of scar tissue in others. The doctors had done multiple skin grafts to try and even out the skin, but my back still looked like a war zone. I could hardly bear to look at it. I didn't want to imagine what Bridget thought.

I was startled from my musings as wetness streaked down my back. I couldn't take the silence anymore.

"I'm sorry. I know they're ugly."

Naked flesh was suddenly pressed up against me as Bridget again engulfed me in her arms. Her entire body shook, and a strangled sob sounded behind me. She squeezed me tightly, as if she would never let me go.

"God, Connor. I can't begin to imagine the pain you must have felt. And don't you dare say your scars are ugly. They're a part of you, and there is nothing about you that is ugly. You are the most beautiful person I know, both inside and out, and I refuse to allow the man I love to degrade himself like that. Do you understand me, Connor Black? Every mark and scar is a testament to your strength. You survived the worst sort of abuse, and yet you're here. You persevered and overcame something most people would never dream of. I am so humbled by you. I know how hard this must have been to show me these. To open yourself up and be vulnerable like that. Thank you for trusting in me. In us."

Her cheek was flush against my back, and I felt her tears on my mangled skin. In my mind, I played back every word she said, trying to decipher her words that somehow didn't make any sense. She wasn't cringing in disgust. I wasn't ugly in her eyes. I tried to take that all in, because my world had just been flipped upside down. And I was pretty sure I'd heard somewhere in there that she loved me. That floored me the most.

"You love me?"

She hiccupped and reined in the tears. I felt my muscles tense as I waited on her answer. She grasped my shoulders and guided me until I was turned around and facing her. Her eyes shone brightly with tears.

"I think I've always loved you, Connor. Even when I didn't have it in me to love someone. You mended a heart I thought broken, never to feel again. A heart that will forever belong to you."

Bridget's words broke the dam of emotions I'd been holding back for years. They flooded my heart and burst through as I grabbed her to me and crashed my mouth down on hers in a bruising kiss. A fever unlike any other came over me, and I couldn't control it. With my hands under her ass, I lifted Bridget and gently laid us back on the bed with her underneath me. Her hands roamed my naked back, and the sensation was out of this world. I was, and always would be, numb in some places where nerve endings would never heal, but here and there, a spark ignited where her hands touched.

I broke the kiss and scanned her face, flushed with arousal. Fuck, I loved this woman. I waited until she opened her eyes before I spoke. When they fluttered open, I stared down at her.

"I can't be gentle right now. I need to fuck you hard, to mark you." Without waiting for a response, I lined my cock up to her wet pussy and thrust to the hilt. Bridget's legs wrapped around my waist, and she pushed herself upward, matching me thrust for thrust. I reached down for one leg and threw it over my shoulder, hitting inside her cunt at a new angle that had her gasping for breath.

"Fuck me, Sir. I'm yours to use any way you want. My body, heart, and soul are yours to do with as you see fit. Fill me. Mark me. Love me."

I couldn't stop, and I couldn't get inside her far enough. I wasn't going to last long this time. I'd more than make it up to her. Each time I withdrew, she squeezed down on my cock, making her pussy tighter. Stars and colors flashed behind my eyes when she did that. My cock swelled, and my balls drew up. I knew I was about to climax. I wanted her to reach her peak with me. I reached between us and rubbed her clit. My jaw was clenched so hard I hoped I didn't break a tooth as I forced my orgasm back. I continued fucking her with an almost punishing strength and then she was screaming her release, her gaze never leaving mine. With one final thrust, my seed erupted inside her and I groaned in satisfaction that I was able to see to my sub's pleasure before mine.

My come dripped out of her soaking wet cunt as I pulled my cock out. I dipped a finger into her, scooped some of it out and began rubbing it all over her gorgeous tits and down her stomach. Bridget was mine, and I wanted everyone to smell me on her skin. I wanted to permanently be a part of her. She grabbed my hand and, staring intently into my eyes, brought my fingers to her mouth, sucking them and licking away every last drop of come. I couldn't stop the words from escaping.

"I love you, Bridget. I want to fuck you raw every night. I want to collar you to show everyone who you belong to. And as much as it scares the fucking hell out of me, I want to make babies with you. I want everything with you."

"I want that too, Sir." she smiled, sleepily.

I lay down and pulled her to me so her back was to my front. I wrapped my arm around her waist and reached up to cup her breast while dropping kisses along her shoulder. After shedding that burden, I was mentally exhausted. I breathed a heavy sigh and finally relaxed, falling into a deep sleep.

CHAPTER 28

THE YOUNG BOY sat cross-legged on the living room floor playing his video game while he waited for his mother to finish cooking his favorite meal, spaghetti and meatballs. He had been riding his bike outside earlier and had removed his shirt due to the stifling heat and was wearing only shorts to help cool off.

He jumped when the crash of the backdoor slamming open sounded from the kitchen, followed by a gruff yell. "Goddamn it. You're not done cooking yet, you stupid bitch?" He'd been conditioned to fear that voice. His heart rate spiked; his palms began to sweat, and tremors racked his body. There was no use hiding. It only made the punishments worse. Best to wait it out and "take it like a man" as he'd been told time and time again. Besides, if it wasn't him, it would be his mother. And he would do whatever he could to protect her.

He'd started growing taller when he turned thirteen last month, but he was still skinny as a rail. Every few nights he would sneak downstairs and eat a little bit of everything. Not enough that someone would notice how much was missing, but enough that he took in more calories in an attempt to grow big and tall so he could protect his mother. But it was no use. No matter how much food he snuck when no one was looking, he was still too small and weak to do anything but survive.

It all started five years ago when his stepfather hurt himself on the job. He started drinking to ease the pain. Once he was healed he went back to work, but didn't stop drinking. He lost job after job because he was drunk. The boy's mother had always been a stay-at-home mom, even before his father died. She had no resources and no way to raise a child, so she said yes to the first man who offered to take care of her. The boy didn't resent her for the choices she'd made.

At first, only his mother had been the recipient of his stepfather's blows. A slap for dinner being late or his clothes not pressed to his liking. The boy, then only eight, tried to intervene, but was then also punished. It began escalating after that. His stepfather drank even more heavily at night and the tiniest infraction set him off. Soon, open-handed slaps turned into fists. Then belts and a few kicks here and there.

When things got really bad, punishments resulted in deep, jagged wounds from belt buckles, small burn scars from cigarettes that marred the boy's chest and back, and striped marks from a switch wielded by a rage-driven hand. The boy never told anyone. Not teachers and not friends who had slowly stopped coming over to play. He was too ashamed and scared. His stepfather threatened to kill his mother if he told. The boy wasn't willing to take that chance. He would do whatever it took to protect her, even accept punishments on her behalf. In the end, though, it hadn't mattered.

Raised voices and then the crack of flesh against flesh sounded from the kitchen, along with a woman's muffled cry. The boy jumped up and raced to the other room, fearful more for his mother than for himself. He skidded to a halt just inside the door. His mother cowered on the floor holding her face, the redness evident through her fingers.

"Leave her alone," the boy yelled. His stepfather's head snapped in his direction, and he could smell the alcohol in the air. The man laughed maniacally, sending chills down the boy's spine.

"What are you going to do about it, boy?" The man taunted, stumbling drunkenly toward the boy. Something inside him snapped at that moment. He'd had enough. He charged the drunkard, ignoring the possible consequences, and head-butted him directly in the gut. The air escaped the man with on "oomph", but caused no more damage than that. Unfortunately, it now left the boy vulnerable and within arms' reach.

Fingernails dug deep into the boy's biceps and he was thrown to the ground in front of the stove. A solid kick to the ribs caused him to cry out in pain. "You little fucker," the man screamed, spittle spewing from his mouth. With the next kick came a cracking noise. The boy huddled in the fetal position cradling his body with his own scrawny arms that offered no protection.

An inhuman scream echoed and a resounding groan bellowed in the air, followed by the sounds of pounding on flesh. The boy looked up to see his mother's useless fists punching the man's back, screams of outrage pouring from her mouth. The man threw the woman off of him, turned, and backhanded her. She fell to the floor next to the broken boy.

The man towered over them, an inferno of hatred blazing from his eyes. "You're both fucking useless," he bellowed. "You," he pointed to the crying, cowering woman, "can't cook for shit. I've told you that dinner was to be ready before I got home, and you can't even fucking get that right."

In his rage, he grabbed the pot of boiling water on the stove and dumped it over the pair. They both wailed from the torturous pain *that riddled their bodies. The boy received the worst of it and the smell of blistered and burnt flesh permeated the air.*

I bolted upright in bed, gasping at the memory while the scars on my back burned. I blinked, slowly orienting myself to my surroundings while wiping the sweat out of my eyes. I glanced down at the sleeping woman next to me, hoping there would be no need to explain why I disturbed her slumber. As luck would have it, Bridget remained oblivious to the mental torment happening right next to her. I couldn't believe she was really here.

God, my throat was dry. I quietly crept out of bed and into the attached bathroom. After running a washcloth under cold water, I wiped away the dried sweat on my face. My reflection stared back at me as I braced my hands on the sink, breathing in deep, calming breaths. Eventually, my heart rate decreased, but I knew there would be no more sleep for me tonight.

I turned out the bathroom light and made my way back to bed, carefully climbing back in, trying not to disturb Bridget. I put my hand under my head and stared at the ceiling still chasing the memories away. Bridget shifted next to me, and I held my breath, hoping she'd stay asleep. Apparently, luck wasn't with me tonight as her eyes blinked open. She shifted closer to me and rested her arm across my chest. As she came more awake, a frown marred her face.

"Your heart is racing. What's wrong?"

I immediately started to deny that anything was wrong, but after last night, I knew I needed to start being more open with her. Old habits were hard to break though.

"Just an old nightmare. It sneaks up on me once in a while. I'm sorry I woke you." I turned onto my side so we were face-to-face, and brushed the hair out of her eyes.

"Do you want to talk about it?" She caressed my chest, drawing tiny circles right above my heart. It felt strange to have skin-to-skin contact with someone, and I knew it would take a while before I got used to the sensation. Bridget leaned forward and placed a gentle kiss on my lips that was a balm to my soul. "You don't have to, you know. But I want to take away your pain and help ease your burdens. I want to be the person you rely on the most. And from the sounds of it, this nightmare is a burden. I'm not pushing you though. If you want to talk about it, I'm here for you, no matter what, Connor. Always. I love you."

CHAPTER 29

"Do you know that you're only the second woman to see my scars? The one and only time I fucked a woman fully naked, she turned away in disgust. I was still conditioned to be this cowardly boy, and it crippled me with insecurities. I had been programmed to think I wasn't good enough. This translated into how I saw myself in other's eyes. Add in that one moment of abhorrence and it set the stage for every sexual encounter I had from that moment forward.

"Every now and then, but even more so since this investigation into Alex started, the memories of the abuse come back. Talking about what happened triggered a nightmare. Everything about that day came back to me. It happens sometimes, but I'm used to it. In truth, I think it makes me more appreciative of everything I have now, including you."

I couldn't resist her. The fact that she'd shed tears for me astounded me. I couldn't remember someone caring this much about me since my mother. It was a lot to wrap my head around. When a person has felt one way for so long, it takes time to break the cycle. And I was ready to break the cycle. I wanted to start a new life with Bridget. And God willing, with Alex. I knew that he was being abused by that piece of shit, but Webber hadn't been able to prove it. It took everything in me not to kill that son of a bitch. I needed to figure out a way to get Alex away from Malcolm permanently, and I needed to figure it out soon. I'd focus on it tomorrow. Right now, my beautiful sub was lying next to me, and my attention needed to be focused solely on her.

"Now, less talking and more fucking."

"But, Sir —"

She squeaked when I rolled us over so I now lay on top of her.

"I said we're done talking, Bridget."

She quickly closed her mouth. I needed to lengthen the leash on the beast a little. I had been reining him in, but I could feel him trying to claw his way out. It terrified me to release him completely though. I'd been a member of Eden long enough to know that there were Doms who enjoyed giving pain and subs who equally enjoyed receiving it. Rationally, I knew there was nothing wrong with that, but there were times when I was afraid I would lose control. That I would take it too far. In the back of my head I heard the laugh of the abusive bastard who used to beat me, taunting me that I was just like him.

I didn't want to hide my true self from Bridget, but I also didn't want to lose her. She'd already chewed my ass once for not communicating with her enough. We had fallen into a pattern where our lust took over. While we had finally discussed limits and I knew her safe word, I had failed in my job as a Dom to trust myself, and most importantly, my sub.

To trust that if what I was doing became too much, she would use her safe word. Now was the time. Especially after the nightmare. It was time to try and banish the ugly thoughts and be true to who I am.

CHAPTER 30

"Don't move."

I slipped off the bed, trusting Bridget to follow my commands. I reached into the top drawer of the nightstand and removed several silken cords and a Kelly green silk scarf. The color was so vibrant, I had immediately pictured Bridget wearing it when I bought it, although I never fully believed she ever would. I placed it over her eyes, holding her head up as I tied it behind her, taking care not to capture any of her hair.

I then carefully pulled out items from the toy box at the foot of the bed, placing everything I thought I was going to need onto a clean towel I kept in the box with them. I wrapped them up and placed them on the bed next to her. I picked up one of her hands and began loosely threading the cord between her fingers and around her palm before securing the cord to the headboard. I repeated the action with her other hand. Then I also bound her legs so she was spread out before me. Distractedly, I unwrapped the towel to access the items I'd gathered.

I took a moment to drink in the sight of her lying there at my mercy. Her pussy glistened in the early morning light that had just begun to light the room. Her nipples puckered, begging for attention. I hated to see them suffer. I took one in my mouth and began nibbling and gently biting, and I released it with a pop. Before she could miss the wet heat, I placed one of the nipple clamps I'd retrieved from the box on it, causing her to gasp at the sensation. Not wanting the other to feel neglected, I repeated the process.

Once both nipples were loosely clamped, Bridget was panting, and I reached for the next implement. I slapped the leather tip of the crop across my palm; the sound reverberating through the room, caused Bridget to jump.

"I told you once I wanted to watch the tears fall as I took a crop to your ass. I want to see the pink darken to red and feel the heat radiate off it. I want to see you writhe and squirm. It'll hurt, and yet you'll take the pain because it pleases me to hurt you. Do you understand, Bridget?"

"Yes, Sir."

"I think I'll wait a little bit for that though. The anticipation only makes it that much sweeter. But I think we need to warm you up a little."

Before I even completed my sentence, I flicked the end across her clamped nipple. It wasn't enough to hurt, but with her nipples already so sensitive, the sensation was magnified. Bridget sucked in air at the first tap. A second flick darted across its twin, this one only slightly harder. I alternated between breasts causing Bridget to moan.

"How does that feel?"

"It stings a little, Sir. But I feel it all the way to my core."

"What color are we?"

"Green, Sir."

Although she couldn't see me, I nodded in approval. "Good girl."

I switched tactics and moved my swats to her inner thigh, narrowly avoiding her pussy. She flinched at the impact, but it was more from surprise. I kept my strikes light enough to not cause much pain, but rather to warm the skin and bring the blood to the surface. I admired the color of her skin as it pinked. I struck at random, sometimes alternating locations, sometimes not.

"Is your pussy wet yet? Does the thought of me causing you pain make you wet?"

"Yes, Sir."

"This pleases me."

Satisfied with the color of her skin, I eyed my target with blatant desire. With a flick of my wrist, I brought the crop down directly on her pussy, still holding back the intensity of my strike.

"Oh my god." She whimpered and half-heartedly struggled against her restraints. *Slap. Slap. Slap.* The vibrations of the corded shaft tickled the palm of my hand. Her clit peeked out from its hood as if in anticipation of the next blow. Her pussy lips darkened in color from light pink to light red, and I reveled in the change. Knowing what I would encounter, I plunged two fingers into her sopping wet cunt. I worked my fingers in and out of her, the wetness coating them.

"Whose pussy is this?"

Her whole body bucked in pleasure as I fucked her with my fingers.

"Yours, Sir." She sounded breathless.

I pulled my glistening fingers out of her and placed them against her lips, coaxing her to taste her own essence.

"Lick. Suck."

She followed my command, lapping up every drop.

I knelt down and inhaled her scent, luxuriating in the smell that was uniquely Bridget. I leaned back to deliver a slashing blow to her pussy causing a pained cry. Before the echo of her cry faded, I sucked her burning clit into my mouth, laving my tongue around it to soothe the ache I'd just created.

"What color?"

"Still green, Sir." This time she was slower to answer, and a soft hiccup sounded behind her words.

Without warning, I reached up with both hands and simultaneously removed the clamps from her nipples, causing her to flinch in pain. I began suckling first one nipple then the other, chasing the pain with pleasure. I moved upward and captured her mouth in a bruising kiss. Our tongues moved together in a coordinated dance. I pulled away, causing her to arch toward me to try and maintain contact.

"Hold still," came my gravelly command, as I reached out to remove the restraints from her wrists, followed by the ones around her ankles. I gently rubbed her wrists, then ankles, making sure the restraints hadn't harmed her.

Finally, I removed the blindfold, finding it wet with tears. I kissed away the single remaining one that had left a wet trail down her cheek.

"Thank you for accepting this pain for me, Bridget. Your complete submission to this need I have means more to me than I can express in words. Hurting you fulfills something inside me I can't explain. At first, I was ashamed of my need to cause pain, to connect pain and pleasure. But because of your love, I feel I can be who I am truly meant to be. That I am free to explore that line between pain and pleasure and move the line that blends pain into pleasure."

She nuzzled my cheek. "I'll accept the pain you have to give me to please you, Sir. I may not understand it, but as your submissive I'm willing to be what you need me to be. The thought of intense pain scares me, but in some way it also arouses me. I love you, Sir. All of you. Even the part that needs to hurt me."

CHAPTER 31

In truth, I *was* both nervous and aroused at the thought of the pain Connor wanted to cause. I never had masochist tendencies before, but then again, none of the Doms I'd played with before were sadists. They hadn't even tried to push my pain limit. Although, I didn't know if Connor actually identified as sadist. Not that it mattered. I loved the man he is. I would do everything I could to fulfill his needs. I was sure it would take some time and a lot of communication, which we both were slowly getting better at.

So far, everything had aroused me tonight. But I knew Connor had barely tested my limits. I knew that I could expect much more. My curiosity about how much pain I could endure was about to be tested as Connor moved away from me.

"We're not done here. Up on your hands and knees. Your ass hasn't felt the bite of the crop yet."

I followed his instructions and waited for further commands. A sigh escaped me as feather light kisses were dropped down the length of my spine. Teasing circles were drawn on my hips, edging closer and closer to my center. Both hands left my hips and the bed shifted. A whoosh of air was all I heard before a sting sizzled across my ass. Although I knew it was coming, I squeaked and jumped in surprise. It hurt, but not overly much. My body actually flushed with arousal.

Connor began a light tapping across my cheeks, not hurting at all, just warming up my skin like he described so many nights ago.

"Ah, the first blush of pink is my favorite."

The taps continued, getting stronger and stronger with each strike until I began flinching. Then they stopped, and a hand began caressing the sting away. My pussy was trained to respond to pleasure and the soft caresses were arousing enough to cause it to weep. Connor's fingers dipped into the wetness.

"Such sweet nectar." Sucking sounds followed his words and although I couldn't see behind me, I pictured him licking my essence off those thick, long digits. More wetness dripped down my thighs at the imagery.

My thoughts were interrupted when another crack of the crop sounded as it made direct contact with my ass. This time though, the strikes quickened and increased in strength until I could no longer stop the flow of tears I didn't realize I was even shedding as the pain increased exponentially. I began sobbing uncontrollably, and just when I reached a point where the pain was intolerable and my safe word was on the tip of my tongue, they stopped. In the same heartbeat, Connor buried his face in my pussy, thrusting his tongue deep inside me, his hands squeezing my ass cheeks to remind me of the pain that still buzzed. He ate at my cunt, sucking and lapping up every drop of my juice. My orgasm came out of nowhere, and I screamed my release.

Before the spasms even ended, Connor's cock entered me and he grabbed my hair, pulling my head back as he rode me hard. He pounded into my aching pussy with an uncontrollable frenzy. With each thrust, the fire reignited across my ass cheeks. But he didn't stop. He reached his hand around and found my clit. He flicked the sensitive nub, causing a shudder to run through me. He circled it with his fingertips and the tremors began again as I climaxed a second time. Connor's roar of satisfaction filled the room, and exhausted, we both collapsed on the bed.

Connor cushioned his descent, and instead of landing directly on top of me, he fell off to the side. I lay on my stomach, my head turned toward him. He shifted onto his side and traced the dried tear tracks down my face.

"Never have I seen anything as beautiful as your tears. You humble me with your submission."

"Thank you for the pain, Sir. It only made the pleasure that much sweeter. For a few brief seconds, the pain and pleasure blended into one giant sensation, and I was no longer able to distinguish one from the other."

Connor pulled me into his arms and hugged me tight, offering me the comfort and care I needed.

"You're mine to care for. I will do my best to cherish and honor your gift of submission."

Heavy with sleep, my eyes closed, and I slept through a dreamless night, content in my Dom's embrace.

CHAPTER 32

THE NEXT MORNING, I woke, sore but satisfied. Everything in my life was coming together. I had Connor, and I hoped to soon have Alex. He and I had talked daily while he was in foster care. He'd been in his foster home for almost two weeks while the investigation was ongoing. For the first week he was away from his uncle, while he didn't sound exactly happy, I could still sense a lightness behind his words as though he'd had a boulder lifted from his shoulders.

But at the beginning of the second week, I'd heard a different tone to his voice when we spoke. I knew he had been worried about having to return home to his uncle. He'd returned to his uncle's house a week ago when they were unable to prove the allegations of abuse. I'd tried reaching him, but anytime I called, his uncle said Alex was unable to come to the phone.

When we had spoken, we'd talked in generalities about seeing how to get some type of visitation. I had originally hesitated to bring it up during one of our many conversations because I didn't know if it was even an option. I needed legal counsel from our friend, Donovan, or to at least get a reference for a lawyer who could help me with this.

I had no intention of mentioning it to Alex, but I wanted to petition for guardianship, and because I had no legal standing, I didn't want to get his hopes dashed. This was another thing I needed to speak to Donovan about. I knew it was going to be almost impossible to gain guardianship, but I knew I needed to try. If not for his sake, then mine. I'd focus on visitation at first and consider going from there.

Then, there was Connor. We had reached a new point in our relationship. We loved each other and wanted a future together. But we hadn't discussed Alex. I hadn't told Connor yet about wanting to pursue guardianship of Alex. I knew Connor cared about him, and I knew he wanted me to be happy, so I was sure he would agree to it. I just didn't know if that was something Alex would want.

Everything with Connor had been amazing this past week. I truly believed that last night and this morning had been a turning point for us. I hated that, after all these years, he still had nightmares, but we both thought that the more he embraced his sadism, the more he'd heal.

I had no doubt he would push my limits in order to fulfill his own needs, but I was willing to do whatever it took to make my Dom happy. I wanted to be the sub he needed. And if what he needed was to push my pain threshold in order to prove to himself that pain and pleasure co-existed, then I'd be there for him. If he needed to prove to himself that he wasn't exactly like that other man, then I'd submit to his demands. Connor could trust in me, and know that I would use my safe word if it became too much. I knew he would find a way to mix pleasure in with the pain.

I had slept half the day and needed to make a quick run to the boutique. I'd been neglecting my store lately, and it didn't sit well with me. I missed being there. I was just about out the door when my cell phone rang. I almost didn't answer it, because of the unknown number on the caller ID, but something told me I should.

"Hello."

"Your broke my fucking nose, you bitch."

"Who is this?"

"Don't worry about who I am right now. Just listen to what I'm telling you. If you want to see your son alive again, you will follow my instructions to the letter. Do you understand?"

"No, I don't understand. What have you done with Alex, you piece of shit?"

"Tsk, tsk. I'd watch what you say to me, whore. If you want your son to remain safe, I'd suggest you be a little bit nicer to me. Now, I won't tell you again. You will follow my explicit instructions, or your son is dead. You will not tell anyone where you're going, and you'll come alone. Once you're in your car, you will shut your phone off. Don't make me explain this again. Now, do you understand?"

"Yes, yes, I understand. Now, please, tell me where you are."

I frantically wrote down the directions he gave me. I wished I had a gun. I'd kill this son of a bitch for threatening my son. I had no idea what this psycho wanted from me, but if I lived through this, Connor was going to kill me for what I was about to do. But I had to go. Alex's life was at risk and nothing would stop me from reaching him. Mama bear had been unleashed and no one would hurt my son.

I ran into the kitchen and grabbed the sharpest knife I

could find. I had no idea if I could really kill someone, but I was going there prepared to do what I had to in order to protect Alex. I made a split second decision, because I knew it would be suicide if I didn't. I had just found my son. I wasn't ready to die yet.

I hurriedly picked up my phone and hit the speed dial button.

"Hey, lady. What's going on with you? How's Connor?"

"Penny, I can't talk long, but I needed someone to know what was going on. I just received a phone call from a man saying he had Alex. He wants me to meet him at some cabin. It was the same man who broke into my house. I'm heading out there now. I've got to go. I love you."

I heard her scream my name in the background as I disconnected the call. I knew going out there, especially alone, was beyond stupid, but it didn't matter. Nothing mattered but Alex.

CHAPTER 33

As I DROVE HOME after speaking with Donovan about what our options were regarding Alex, I couldn't stop my mind from returning to last night. I had never before felt as much myself as I did with Bridget. Embracing my true self had been freeing and cathartic. A weight had been lifted from my shoulders.

I looked down at my phone, which had begun ringing. I wondered what Marcus wanted.

"Hey, man, what's up?"

"We have a problem. Bridget just called Penny and said she'd received a call from the same man who broke into her apartment. Connor, he has Alex. And Bridget is going after them."

"God damn it! Please tell me she didn't go alone? Did she, I don't know, happen to mention where the hell she was going?"

"She mentioned a cabin, but that was it. Nothing about where it was. I'm sorry."

"Of course she didn't. She couldn't have made this easy

for me. Typical Bridget. Thanks, Marcus. Please let me know if she calls Penny again." I disconnected the call and immediately called Webber, who answered on the first ring.

"I need your help."

Webber must have sensed the urgency in my voice, because he didn't give me any shit about having to come to him for something.

"What's wrong?"

I explained to him what Marcus had told me. I knew it was a long shot, but I needed him to try and track her phone. I told him to call me back if he could find anything out. In the meantime, I made a detour and headed straight to Malcolm's house. Just as I reached the house, Webber called me back with exactly what I knew he'd say. Bridget's phone had been turned off. We were in the dark. I swore to God this woman would be the death of me.

"Webber, you might want to get over here. It looks like Shipman's had company before me. The door is partially open. I'm heading in."

"Stay put, Black. I don't need you contaminating a possible crime scene. I'll be there shortly."

"I don't give a fuck about your crime scene. These are Bridget and Alex's lives we're talking about. I need to see if I can find anything in here that will help me locate them quickly. They're in danger, and I'm not waiting on you." I hung up without waiting for a response.

Everything inside me told me that Malcolm was behind this. I mentally reviewed everything I had discovered about him. Nothing came to mind about a remote cabin. I needed to find it and soon. I pushed the door until it opened fully. I needed to see if I could find any clues.

Cautiously, I made my way inside. The first room I came

to was the living area, where total destruction lay before me. Papers were strewn everywhere, tables turned over, couch cushions slit. Someone had obviously been looking for something. What I didn't know was whether it had been before or after Bridget went after Alex.

I stepped carefully over the debris on the floor and made my way to other areas of the house, hoping to find something I could use to locate my family. And Bridget and Alex were my family. When nothing in the bedrooms offered any clues, I returned to living room where the majority of ruin was located. I picked up random pieces of paper and examined each of them. When I couldn't find anything that even looked like it would remotely help, I made a phone call.

Immediately, she picked up.

"Josephine speaking."

"Josie, I need you to work your magic. And I need you to do it, like, yesterday."

"No problem, boss, whatcha need?"

"Malcolm Shipman. I know you looked into his bank records for me already, but there must be something you missed. I need to see if he owns some type of cabin. I don't know where, and I can't give you any more information than that."

I actually cringed when I inferred she might have overlooked something. Josie didn't miss anything.

"I didn't find anything, sir, but let me take another look. Give me a sec."

The rat-a-tat sound of fingers on a keyboard echoed loudly in the background. I could see her sitting at her desk, her dual computer screens in front of her, her glasses almost falling off the tip of her nose.

I met Josephine Bishop when she was a fresh-faced teen.

She had just started her first year at MIT. She was a computer genius and the daughter of a former client. I hired her immediately after graduation, and it was one of the best career decisions I'd ever made. I never asked where she learned to hack into organizations whose firewalls and security were state of the art. I'd utilized her hacking skills more than once, and she was one of the best.

"I think I found something, sir. It wasn't something I would have found if I hadn't been specifically looking for it. Malcolm Shipman's paternal grandfather purchased some land about sixty years ago. It's a small strip, about five acres, approximately forty miles outside of town, halfway up the mountain. The reason why it didn't show up during my initial review of Malcolm Shipman's assets is because the property actually belongs to Christopher and Malcolm Shipman's aunt, Mabel Shipman. It was passed down to her by her father. She never married and had no children. There is a small cabin on the property. No one actually lives there, but it looks like it garners some income as a rental property. It's situated right on the river and is used as a weekend retreat for fly fisherman. It might be the place you're looking for. I've dug as deep as I can possibly dig, sir."

"Thank you for your hard work, Josie. I need you to text me the location of the cabin. Also, I need you to get Miles on the phone. Let him know I need him there. I'm on my way to the cabin now."

I hung up the phone and raced out to my car. If any harm had come to Bridget or Alex, I was going to kill Malcolm.

CHAPTER 34

THE SINGLE-STORY CABIN sat about a hundred feet off the road, partially hidden behind some trees with a view of the mountains behind it. It was bigger and better kept than I expected. There were two steps leading up to the large wrap-around porch where two white, high back rocking chairs sat. A white, wooden swing hung from the porch awning. A small landscaped area graced the border around the porch and was dotted with multi-colored flowers. If I weren't so afraid for Alex, I could appreciate the gorgeous view in front of me.

The minute I exited my car, I could hear water flowing from a creek or river nearby. I loved coming to the mountains during the fall, but I certainly didn't want to be here under the current circumstances. I had done as instructed and turned my cell phone off the minute I got in my car. Whoever had Alex was either dumb to assume I'd actually do it or had put an awful lot of faith in the fact that I would follow his instructions. Regardless, I didn't want to take any chances, so I played by his rules.

I slowly walked toward the house, constantly on the lookout for someone who might jump out of the bushes. With every step, I could feel the small knife shift where it was tucked in my back waistband. I prayed it didn't fall out or that I didn't accidentally stab myself. A bead of sweat trickled between my breasts, and I was on the verge of throwing up from nerves and fear.

I hadn't even reached the steps before the door opened and a man I didn't recognize stepped out on the porch. He looked only slightly taller than me with short, salt and pepper hair. He was average looking with two black eyes, the colored bruises faded. I'd never seen such hate emanating from someone. There was also a crazed look in his eyes that left me trembling in fear. Crazy people were even more dangerous. This man had the look of someone who had reached the end of his rope. I only prayed he didn't do anything drastic. People with nothing left to lose did desperate things.

"You followed my instructions, correct?"

I had to clear my throat before I could answer. "Tell me where Alex is. Is he safe? Please, I'm begging you."

"You aren't the one asking the questions here, bitch. Now, answer me."

"Yes, yes, I came alone, and didn't tell anyone where I was going. My phone is off and in my car. I answered your questions, now please, I need to know if Alex is here and that he's safe."

"Get inside, now."

Needing answers, but not wanting to piss him off too much, I hurried up the steps and into the house, the man following behind me. Once inside, I immediately spotted Alex tied to a chair, hands behind his back and his feet tied to the legs of the chair, a gag in his mouth, and a bruise already forming around his eye. The second he saw me, he screamed behind the gag and struggled to get free of his bindings. I cried out as I raced over to him and pulled the gag off his mouth.

"Alex, honey, are you all right?" Tears clogged by throat as I cupped his cheeks.

"I'm okay."

"Are you sure?"

"I promise, I'm fine."

Without a thought to the consequences and acting on instinct only, I turned and threw myself at this asshole who had hit my child. I caught him off guard and clipped his jaw, but he recovered quickly. He grabbed my hair and punched me in the face. I fell to the floor from the impact, leaving strands of hair in his grasp.

"You fucking bitch. I should kill you for that. Better yet, I'll let you watch as I kill the kid over there."

"No, please, I won't do it again. I'll do anything you say, just leave Alex alone." Blood dripped down my lip and splashed onto the floor. My side was killing me too. I hadn't fully healed from the last beating this man had given me. And I still didn't know who he was.

I slowly picked myself up off the floor, warily eyeing him to make sure he wasn't going to strike again. When he remained where he was, I stepped away and moved over to crouch next to Alex as I wrapped my arm around him. "Who are you? Why are you doing this?" I begged for answers.

"He's my uncle," Alex answered for him.

Aghast, I stared. This was Alex's uncle? The man who'd been abusing him? He hadn't answered my question about why though. What had prompted this man to kidnap and threaten to kill us?

"Why?" I asked again.

He shrugged, seemingly unconcerned. "I owe a lot of money to some very bad people. Because this little bastard called you, the police started nosing around in my affairs. My access to the money was cut off during the investigation, and the people I owe money to don't give an extension on payment due. So, unless I pay them what they're owed, they're going to kill me. And it's all your fault. You couldn't leave well enough alone. You had to sic your musclehead boyfriend on me. Now, you're both going to pay. First, I'm going to kill you. Then, I'm going to kill your boyfriend. Once you're both out of the picture, the police will stop bothering me. I'll be able to pay what I owe, and everything will be okay then."

He walked over to the kitchen island that butted up against the border of the kitchen and living room, and that was when I saw the gun. He picked it up and tilted it back and forth in his hand before opening the chamber to examine the bullets inside. I felt sick to my stomach.

All I thought to myself was that this couldn't be happening. I could only stare in shock at this lunatic who thought he could murder two people and get away with it. He clearly had no idea who Connor was. Or the friends he had. They wouldn't rest until they'd found his killer. Alex's uncle was crazy. Completely and utterly bat shit crazy.

"Do you really think you're going to get away with that? Connor is friends with a police detective. If he goes missing, they're going to investigate. Fingers are going to be pointed at you." I wasn't intentionally trying to poke the bear. The bear with the gun. I just couldn't seem to help myself. I only hoped it wouldn't lead to my death.

"If I don't pay, Louie Falcone will kill me. I'd rather take my chances with you than him. I'm guaranteed to be feeding the fishes if Mr. Falcone doesn't get his money."

I really wished Connor were here. I hoped and prayed the whole way here that Penny had passed on my message. I didn't know what kind of skillsets the people working for Connor had, but I imagined they had to be phenomenal at their jobs for him to be as successful as he was. I was putting an awful lot of faith in Connor. But I knew he'd do everything in his power to find us. I just needed to keep Alex and myself alive until then. Inconspicuously, I reached behind me to make sure the knife was still where I'd hidden it. I breathed a sigh of relief when I felt it beneath my fingertips. A knife didn't have a chance against a gun, but it was my only option. I had been scanning the place since I'd sat next to Alex, looking for some type of weapon I could use besides my puny knife. I was kicking myself for not spotting the gun sooner. I could have used it to my advantage had I known it was there. But my main focus had been on Alex.

After hearing Malcolm's plans for me, I knew, without a doubt, that if it came down to him or me, there would be no hesitation on my part. I would defend myself in any way I could, and if I killed him the process, so be it. I tensed when Malcolm started pacing the length of the floor. He didn't appear to be paying attention to us, but I knew that it was only a matter of time before he made his move.

CHAPTER 35

THE HOUR or so drive to the Shipmans' cabin was the longest sixty minutes of my life. By my estimation, Bridget had been there for a couple of hours already. I prayed like I had never prayed before that I made it to the cabin before Malcolm hurt either of them. I was still trying to understand his motive for taking such desperate measures. Considering the amount of money he owed Mr. Falcone, my guess would be fear. Fear was always a motivating factor when people did crazy things.

I knew Miles would be right behind me, so when I finally reached the vicinity of the cabin, I pulled off on the side of the road, left the car there, and began my trek the rest of the way to the cabin. I didn't want to give away the fact that I was here. After about fifteen minutes of walking, I came across the driveway. I snuck along the drive, staying close to the trees to conceal my arrival as best I could. As soon as I moved around the last tree, I spotted Bridget's car. I didn't realize how scared I had been, not knowing whether this was exactly where Bridget had come. I breathed a small sigh of relief.

A soft rustling sounded behind me. I withdrew my gun and waited. When Miles peeked around the corner, I relaxed. Miles had been in my employ since the second year I opened Blacklight Securities. He was, in fact, my second-in-command. I trusted him more than I trusted anyone. Well, besides Bridget now. He'd been a good friend throughout the years.

Miles came to stand next to me. "Have you seen anything yet?"

"Nothing. You arrived right behind me so I haven't had the chance to get closer and scope anything out. All is quiet."

"Do you have a plan?"

"My only plan is to not get Bridget or Alex killed. I need eyes inside that cabin. To see what we're up against. I'm going to see if I can get around back by heading through these trees. I want you to stay here and wait for my signal."

Not waiting for an answer, because I knew Miles would follow my instructions to the letter, I set off through the trees, staying close to the outside to keep the house in view. After dodging branches and other foliage, I finally reached the back of the house. I crept out of the woods, and ducking low, I raced to the house and leaned against it, staying out of view of the windows. I quickly snuck a glance into the nearest one. Inside was a bedroom. The bed was still made, and I could clearly see one door led into a bathroom. The other door appeared to lead out into a hallway.

I ducked under the window and kept creeping along the wall until I reached the side of the house. Again, I peeked into the window and stopped in my tracks. The window was in the kitchen, but with the open floor plan, I was able to see the living room as well. Malcolm was pacing back and forth, a gun in his hand, and with each pass, I caught a glimpse of Bridget and Alex. What I saw pissed me off. Bridget was sitting on her knees on the floor, her hand on Alex's leg. A bruise was forming on her face and her lip was split. Again. Her lip had only just recently closed up. Alex was tied to a kitchen chair and had a black eye and who knew what other injuries. Both of them looked terrified with tear tracks running down their faces.

Bridget sat awkwardly, her side hurting. I saw red at the thought that Malcolm had caused further injury. I needed to formulate a plan. So far, everything appeared calm, but I had no idea if Malcolm would go off at any second. I had to stop myself from charging in. I didn't want to rush in and put them into further danger. I don't know if she sensed my eyes on her or not, but at that moment Bridget looked up and our eyes connected. I saw her gasp, and I quickly ducked back and away from the window.

I heard Malcolm start yelling. "What did you see out there? Is someone here?" And then louder, "Is that you Connor? I have your whore and her bastard in here. You just made my job easier. I don't have to wait to kill you. I get a two for one here."

Miles was still out there, waiting. I signaled to him I was going in and he needed to be ready when the time came. I made my way to the front of the house and stood pressed against the wall next to the front door. I tucked my gun in the waistband of my pants at the small of my back. Then, I called out a warning before I slowly started to open the door.

"I'm coming in."

Through the crack in the door, I slowly stuck my head in,

hoping he didn't blow it off. I kept my eyes on him as I stepped fully inside. Hoping Malcolm didn't notice, I kept the door cracked open for Miles and attempted to distract him. I put my hands above my head to show him I wasn't a threat.

"What are you doing, Malcolm? Do you think you're going to get away with this?"

"I have no other choice. If it weren't for the two of you poking your nose in my business, then none of this would have had to happen. I need that money from the trust. Mr. Falcone will kill me otherwise."

"What makes you think I won't kill you first?"

He swung the gun in Bridget and Alex's direction and cocked it. "Because those two are my insurance policy."

My body froze when he aimed the gun in their direction. I needed to keep him talking, distracted, and away from the door where I knew Miles was making his way to. But first, I needed to check on my woman. Keeping my hands where he could see him and without breaking eye contact, I slowly walked in their direction, making sure I didn't show him my back. When I reached them, Bridget stood and both of us moved to stand in front of Alex to block him with our bodies.

"Are you all right, baby?" I wiped the tears that had begun to fall.

"I knew you'd find me," she whispered.

"Always, love. You know that when we get out of here, I'm going to spank your ass raw for not only coming here alone but for not even contacting me first before you set out on this harebrained scheme." I spoke softly so Alex couldn't hear.

She laughed quietly in spite of her tears. "I'd expect nothing less, Sir."

I looked down at Alex. "What about you, son? You okay? You're not hurt anywhere else are you?"

He shook his head. "No, sir."

"I'm going to get us out of here. I promise." I winked to try and reassure him.

I turned my head to face Malcolm again. As I did, I saw a shadow pass in front of the door. I knew Miles was in place.

"Let me untie Alex. He's just a little boy. You're the one with the gun. The one in control. But I need to make sure he's okay. So, let me untie him."

"No. He's fine right where he is. Now, I need you to step away from them."

"I don't think so."

Just then, Miles burst through the door, gun drawn. "Drop it."

Startled, Malcolm swung around, taking his eyes off us. "Stay back. I swear I'll shoot them."

Miles remained collected as he issued his order again. "I said, drop the gun, Shipman."

Malcolm's eyes darted between Miles and me, Bridget, and Alex. A crazed look flashed across his face, and at that moment I knew he then realized he wasn't going to get his revenge. He turned fully to me and raised his gun, intent on taking at least one of us down.

Without hesitation, Miles fired. Malcolm screamed out in pain and fell to the floor, clutching his leg as blood poured out of the wound. I breathed a sigh of relief that it was over. Now that Malcolm was down, my focus shifted back to Bridget and Alex. Bridget hadn't wasted any time; she was already hurriedly untying Alex. Once he was free, she immediately threw her arms around him and crushed him to her. Both of them burst into tears. Bridget glanced over at me and suddenly a look of terror crossed her face.

"Connor!" Bridget screamed out a warning. I quickly turned to see Malcolm raise the gun from the floor and point it straight at us. Even knowing I'd never reach it in time, I tried grabbing my gun from behind my back at the same time I pushed her and Alex out of the way. A gunshot sounded, and I braced myself for the pain, expecting to feel a bullet explode through me.

The echo of the gunshot faded, and I remained standing. Opening eyes I hadn't realized were closed, I saw Malcolm lying on the floor, a large puddle of blood forming under his head. My eyes shot up to Miles who held a still smoking gun in his hands. He stood immobile, face pale, hands shaking, but his stare never left the now dead body on the floor.

I frantically raced over to Bridget and Alex to make sure neither was hurt.

"Are either of you hit?"

Alex was completely dazed, but Bridget was holding her composure better than I expected.

"We're both fine, I swear."

After I was reassured that they hadn't been injured, I slowly walked over to Miles and gently pried the gun from his clenched fingers. I put my arm around him and guided him over to a kitchen chair, forcing him to sit. He had a glazed expression; he was clearly in shock knowing he'd just killed a man. We'd seen dead bodies in our line of work, but this was the first time he'd caused the death of another human being.

I knelt directly in front of him. "Look at me, Miles," I

demanded. He never even blinked. I tried again, my tone sharper this time. "Miles."

His head snapped in my direction and his eyes met mine. "It's over. We're okay." He shook himself and then nodded slowly at me. Knowing there was nothing else I could do for him and knowing that Bridget and Alex were safe, I pulled out my phone and dialed Webber's number.

CHAPTER 36

WHEN MALCOLM HAD POINTED his gun at Connor, I knew he was going to kill him. I'd never been so scared in all my life. And the blood. Oh my god. I refused to let go of Alex and kept his eyes averted from the body on the floor. Connor was speaking to his friend, a man I'd seen that first day at Connor's office, which seemed like a lifetime ago. The dazed expression on his face surely matched the one on my own.

I watched as Connor led him into the kitchen. They briefly spoke before Connor was pulling out his phone. Needing to get Alex out of this room, I held his hand and brought him with me into the kitchen.

"Alex and I are going into the bedroom. He doesn't need to see — " I didn't know what to say. His uncle? The dead body? Regardless of how it was phrased, it couldn't be easy to reconcile the fact that his uncle had tried to kill us.

"Hold on." Connor spoke into the phone. "Do I need to come with you? Webber can wait."

"No, we'll be fine. Talk to Detective Webber."

Connor nodded and I heard his "All right, I'm here. We

have a problem." as I guided Alex to the back of the house, continuing to keep him out of direct sight of the living room.

Once we reached the bedroom, I sat Alex on the bed. He still hadn't said a word. He wasn't even crying. I first checked his arms and hands to make sure they weren't bleeding from the ropes. Then, I knelt down to take off his shoes. I pulled up each leg of his jeans and checked each of his legs as well. There was a little redness around his wrists, but no broken skin.

"Why don't you lay down sweetie." He continued to sit there listlessly. I gently nudged him and when he didn't fight me, I laid him down myself. When I moved away for a second, he grabbed my hand.

"Don't leave me." My heart ached at his broken tone.

I squatted down next to him. "I'm not leaving, baby. I was just going to find a blanket."

He shook his head and refused to let go of my hand.

"I'm right here, love. I'm not going anywhere." Not knowing what else to do, I scooted him over and crawled into the bed next to him. The second I wrapped my arms around him, he burst into gut-wrenching sobs. I hugged him to me tightly, doing my best to comfort him. Eventually, his sobs quieted to soft hiccups. I listened as his breathing evened out and he fell into an exhausted sleep. I waited a little while to make sure he didn't wake before I quietly slipped out of the bed and made my way back out front. The couch blocked my view of the living room floor. I wasn't surprised to see Detective Webber had arrived and was standing in the kitchen speaking with Connor. Connor's friend was nowhere to be found.

He nodded when I entered the room and came to stand next to Connor. "Bridget."

"Detective Webber."

Dreading it, but doing it anyway, I quickly glanced into the living room, and saw that Alex's uncle's body was still there, but someone had covered it up. I stood there, feeling like I should be doing something. I wasn't used to being idle. Connor put his arm around me and pulled me close.

"Connor has filled me in a little on what happened here. I need to know what happened before Connor got here though, Bridget."

Thinking back on everything that had happened today, I couldn't believe it had only been this morning that I'd been trying to figure out how to try and get guardianship of Alex. And now his uncle was dead. Holy shit. I gave Daniel the details while he took notes and asked an occasional question.

"You know what happened next."

Webber nodded. "Yes, Connor explained his version of the story from the time he arrived. I've called the coroner to come and collect the body, and the sheriff's office as well as county CSI should be here any minute to go over the crime scene. I recommend that you guys go ahead and stay in the bedroom and out of the way. Also, we have our suspicions about who the corrupt cop was that falsified the report on the Shipman's death. She's under investigation. I thought you'd want to know. There isn't anything more I need from either of you at the moment, but you will need to make sure that you are both available for any further questions I might have."

He started to turn, but paused partway as though remembering something. He stared intently into my face. "I'm really glad you're safe, Bridget." He turned and quickly walked out of the house to wait for the other officers to arrive.

Connor's hand felt warm in mine as he led me back to the bedroom where Alex still slept.

"Where did your friend go?"

"Miles? I sent him outside. He should be, if he followed my orders, on the phone with a friend of mine. He needs someone to talk to right now. To take his mind off everything."

"I understand. I don't think I told you this, but thank you for saving us. He was going to kill me and then go after you. He blamed all of us, even Alex, for losing access to the trust. I had no idea what he was even talking about. He was totally insane."

Connor looked over at Alex to make sure he was still asleep. He spoke softly.

"Malcolm was siphoning money out of the trust to pay off his gambling debts. I can't prove it, but I suspect that Malcolm had Alex's parents killed. And when Alex contacted you initially, it started a chain of events that put Malcolm under the spotlight. He was investigated, which is how the disappearing money was discovered. He would have had legal troubles regardless of our involvement, especially when the money started to run out. He would have had to kill Alex to claim his insurance money. The death of three family members that close together would have raised a dozen red flags. There was no way he would have gotten away with any of it. His troubles would have happened sooner rather than later anyway."

"So, what happens now?"

"With what?"

"This. Us. Everything."

"Nothing's changed for me, Bridget. I love you and want to spend the rest of my life with you. Isn't that what you still want?"

Connor still had one of my hands in his so I grabbed his other one and held tight. "God, yes, Connor. More than anything. I love you too, and nothing would make me happier than spending my life with you. There is just one thing. I hadn't said anything to you yet, because I wasn't sure what your thoughts were, but I want to do everything I can to get custody of Alex. Especially now."

"Absolutely. I had every intention of contacting Donovan and getting his advice. Alex holds a piece of my heart too. Not only because he's a great kid, but because he's a part of you. There is nothing I won't do for either of you. Nothing."

I leaned up and placed a soft kiss on his lips, falling even more in love with this man. I don't know how I ever got so lucky.

Suddenly, Alex, in the throes of a nightmare, cried out from the bed. I jerked away and rushed over and crawled into the bed with him and tried my best to soothe him. Connor moved the chair from across the room to place it next to the bed. He took a seat and reached for my hand, lacing our fingers, and forming a connection between the three of us.

CHAPTER 37

DONOVAN, Connor, and I sat outside the courtroom waiting for the judge to let us know whether I would be granted guardianship of Alex or not. It had been three weeks since Malcolm's death, and there was no one else besides his adoptive great-aunt who was willing to take responsibility for him, even though her willingness to accept responsibility only extended so far as to possibly transfer custodial guardianship to me. It would break my heart if the judge refused my petition and, instead, sent Alex into foster care permanently.

Alex was still having nightmares on occasion, but we talked every day and spent weekends together. He had started seeing a therapist so he had someone he could talk to besides me, and he was slowly starting to heal. He still had a long road ahead of him.

I hoped it helped my case now that Connor and I were engaged. An engaged woman had a better chance than a single woman, right? I prayed like I had never prayed before. The door to the courtroom opened, and I jumped in excitement and nervousness. I sagged against Connor in disappointment when I saw it wasn't Alex's *Guardian ad Litem,* Ms. Jackson. I had never been a patient person anyway, so this waiting was driving me insane. I was ready to tear out my hair. Unable to sit still any longer, I quickly stood and began pacing.

After ten minutes of pacing and still no sign of life exiting the courtroom, Connor finally spoke. "Bridge, walking a hole in the floor isn't going to make things happen any more quickly."

I flashed him a look of irritation. "I know that, but it's helping me burn off this excess energy. I can't sit still. Do you not understand that those people in there have control over my future? I know they're supposed to have Alex's best interests at heart, but these people know nothing about me. Yet they get to decide if I'm fit to raise my own son. It's terrifying. So, if I need to pace to keep my sanity, then damn it, I'm going to pace…Sir." I added, belatedly.

Connor took pity on me and my terse words and just shook his head. The next time I paced close enough to him, he reached out, grabbed my hand, and pulled me down onto his lap. I struggled for only a second, until his grip tightened, and he stopped me with a single command.

"Sit."

I narrowed my eyes. "I'm not a dog, Connor."

"No, you're not. But you are my woman, and I told you to sit still. Just put your head on my shoulder and relax. You're getting yourself all worked up and as your fiancé, it's my job to make sure you are being taken care of. So, sit on my lap like the nice little sub that I know you can be and just relax. They'll come out when they're ready and not a minute sooner. I know you're anxious and antsy. I completely understand. I want you to know that no matter what their decision is, I love you and we'll get through this. Together."

I sighed in temporary contentment at his words as I rested my head on his broad shoulder. I had finally figured out why his shoulders were so wide. He carried everyone's burdens. I loved this man more than I ever thought I could. He'd helped heal my broken heart and taught me that I could love again. I knew our relationship would take work. We were both extremely stubborn people. But we complemented each other so well it was scary. I was jarred from my musings by a voice coming from the slightly ajar courtroom door.

"Mr. Jeffries, Judge Beckman will see you and your clients now."

I leapt off Connor's lap so quickly I almost tumbled to the floor. He reached out to steady me. Once I had my balance, I focused on the judge's clerk holding the door open. I wanted to appear calm and collected, but I knew I hadn't succeeded as I hurried over to her. She stepped aside and motioned for the three of us to enter. Donovan led the way. The room closed in on me, seeming to shrink in size since we had last been in here just a few short hours ago. I controlled my breathing by taking slow, deep breaths in and letting them out twice as slow.

"If you'd all like to take a seat over there," the clerk directed us to the long table at the front of the room, "court will reconvene in just a moment."

I scurried over to the table with Connor and Donovan following behind me. I sat and immediately started bouncing my knee in impatience. The woman exited through the door to the side of the judge's bench.

Not five minutes passed before the door opened again,

this time bringing two people into the room. The judge and Ms. Jackson took their seats on the bench and at the table respectively, as if they didn't have a care in the world. As though my life didn't hang in the balance. They took their time settling in and Ms. Jackson slowly began pulling papers out of her briefcase. I ground my jaw to stop from screaming at them to get their shit in gear.

Finally, they acknowledged us. It was the judge who addressed me. "Ms. Carter, I have reviewed your petition to transfer guardianship of the minor, Alex Gregory Shipman, to you from a Ms. Mabel Shipman. I have taken into consideration the written statement provided by Ms. Shipman regarding her inability to raise the young boy at this time. I have interviewed Alex and taken his wishes into consideration. Ms. Jackson has also spoken to Alex as well as made every attempt to locate another family member who would be willing to take guardianship of him without success.

"In cases like this, it is always a difficult decision, because we have to do what is in the best interest of the child. Therefore, we did not make our decision lightly. The court understands why you gave Alex up for adoption and terminated your parental rights fourteen years ago. We commend your motives to do what you felt was best for your child at the time."

The judge paused, and my heart dropped. My palms were sweaty, and I was having trouble catching my breath. I was on the verge of a full-blown panic attack. I barely felt Connor's hand clasp mine tightly.

The judge continued, "In spite of your termination of your parental rights, you acted as a mother when your son was in trouble. You put him first and did what you could to keep him safe. Perhaps you should have spoken to the police first instead of Mr. Black here, but I understand why you chose the path you did. Based on our interviews with all the parties involved as well as your friends, family, and neighbors, I have approved your petition and hereby grant your petition for permanent guardianship of the minor child, Alex Gregory Shipman, effective immediately."

The buzzing in my ears drowned out his words, so it took me a few minutes to process exactly what he'd said. I sat in numbed silence until Connor nudged me, snapping me out of my dazed fog.

Stunned, all I could get out was, "Are you serious?"

Finally, both Judge Beckman and Ms. Jackson smiled. The judge answered, "Yes, Ms. Carter, Alex is now your legal ward. The clerk will have the signed order for you shortly, and one of the bailiffs will bring Alex to you in a few minutes. Congratulations and best of luck to all of you. This court is adjourned."

The tears rolled down my cheeks as soon as the judge said yes. I missed everything he said after that. Luckily, Donovan was there to take care of all the formal details. Just then, the door in the back of the courtroom opened and in walked my son. I rushed over to him and wrapped my arms around him in the tightest hug while I cried joyful tears. Warmth surrounded me when I felt a set of arms embrace us. I absorbed Connor's strength. Eventually, I pulled away and wiped Alex's tears from his face.

I stared into the beautiful face so much like mine. "I love you so much. I'll do everything I can to be the best mom I can be."

"I love you too, Mom," he said, almost bashfully as he tried out the new title. Fresh tears began at the sound of that single word. Alex turned to Connor and spoke.

"Thank you for everything, sir."

Connor nodded and ruffled Alex's hair with a burst of laughter. "You don't have to call me sir. And I'm glad I could be there for you, kid. Now, how about we get out of here?"

Judge Beckman's clerk pointed to the paperwork on the desk and said, "We just need Ms. Carter to sign some forms which will only take a moment, and then you are all free to go. You'll receive the final order by registered mail."

Donovan had already looked over the paperwork and assured us that everything looked good. I hurriedly signed my name to the forms they needed today. When I finished, and the clerk handed over the envelope with the order, I reached for Alex and Connor's hands, and we walked out of the courthouse to start our new life as a family.

Thank you for reading! I hope you enjoyed meeting Connor and Bridget. The next book in the Dom of Club Eden series is REDEMPTION. Miles can't get over killing a man and is haunted by his ghost. Josephine knows her love will heal his heart, if only he'd just see her.

Buy REDEMPTION today or read it for FREE in Kindle Unlimited.
http://amzn.to/2s7scmZ

And if you enjoyed DESIRE, you'll love the sexy, suspenseful IN TOO DEEP. Buy it today or read for FREE in Kindle Unlimited: https://amzn.to/2lVn0BB

Thank you for reading **DESIRE**. Whether you loved it or

hated it, it would be amazing if you would please leave a review on BookBub or your favorite retailer. Reviews are the lifeblood of an author. They help by spreading word about the book and improving visibility so others have the opportunity to read it. In this world of ever increasing self-published authors, visibility is paramount.

Want a FREE short story? Be sure to sign up for her newsletter and download your copy of A Birthday Spanking, a Doms of Club Eden prequel! http://bit.ly/LKShawNewsletter

Turn the page for a short excerpt from REDEMPTION

REDEMPTION

HE THOUGHT I couldn't see the pain in his eyes, but I did. I saw everything about Miles Standish. I always have, even from that the moment I first spied him across the break room. My gaze followed him everywhere, even when I tried to force myself to look away. I'd never met a man before that affected me the way Miles did. I'd been in love with him all these years, but nothing I did swayed him to change our relationship. For six years this man had fought his attraction to me and never once made a move. He could try the patience of a saint. I showed him every way I knew how that I cared for him. Deeply.

Several of my girlfriends, who I'd casually mentioned Miles to in passing, asked me why I didn't ask him out, didn't take the initiative, especially given my proclivity of being rather "take charge". The partial answer to that was that I was, thanks to my father, still gun-shy about trusting men outside the kink community, even Miles. The other answer, the one that had me more hesitant, was that I was a Domme, and being a sexually dominant woman in a vanilla world was difficult. Some men were touchy about submitting to a woman. I had very specific tastes, and there was no sense risking a broken heart on a man who wasn't who I needed him to be.

For that reason, I didn't try to push, even as heat simmered in his eyes when he thought I wasn't looking. But now, other emotions clouded Miles' eyes. Pain. Guilt. My heart broke for him.

It's been six years since that first day on the job, and Miles still sent shivers down my spine with every look, every touch. Now though, I also knew one additional thing about him. I knew he'd killed a man. A man who, like the one I'd killed, deserved to die.

I saw how it affected him. Gone was the lightheartedness. No longer did he prop his butt on the corner of my desk and joke with me. I recognized the guilt that ate at him, even if I'd never experienced it myself. I didn't regret, for one second, killing that bastard. I also recognized the signs of someone going through the motions of existing but not living. My sister was a member of that club. It broke me knowing that I couldn't do anything to help her. But I'd be damned if I wouldn't do everything in my power to help Miles get rid of the guilt. Somehow, I'd find a way to bring him back from the darkness that shrouded him. I loved him too much to fail.

Chapter 2 - Miles

BLOOD. It's everywhere. It doesn't matter if I'm awake or asleep. All I see is blood. And his face. I brushed my teeth this morning, and when I leaned up from the sink, there he stood, behind me, staring at me with blood running down his face. Rationally, I knew he wasn't there. Except it's hard to be rational since I'd started losing my mind months ago. I knew it was happening, but there was nothing I could do to stop it. It's hard to tell my mind it's playing tricks on me. Especially when guilt for the very death I caused overwhelms me.

Malcolm Shipman deserved to die. He'd been on the verge of pulling the trigger of his own gun when I'd shot him to save the life of my boss. My best friend. One of the two was going to die. I'd chosen Malcolm. I've been to the shooting range countless times. I've run through mock hostage situations where I've shot dummies scattered around the room at almost point-blank range. It never occurred to me that shooting another human being, regardless of whether he deserved it or not, would change a person as drastically as it's changed me.

I still go to the gym and to work every day. I talk to my co-workers and occasionally, I try to laugh at their jokes. But even I can hear the hollowness behind my laughter. Behind my words. Life around me has moved forward, and no one knows what's going on behind my false gaiety. Except *her*. I've been avoiding her ever since that day, because I can't take the pity in her eyes. She tries to hide it, but I see it. Along with several other emotions that I've known were there for years. Hope. Attraction. Love, perhaps. But none of those shone so brightly as pity.

Josephine Bishop showed up one day, and my life has never been the same. I've stayed away from her for several reasons, not the least of which is she's fifteen years my junior. I knew she was infatuated with me when she first joined the team, and I did everything I could to give her the impression I wasn't interested. Eventually, she reeled her emotions back in and treated me like a friend. Our morning talks have always been my favorite part of the day, even if I didn't admit it to anyone.

She was a conundrum. She possessed both an aura of innocence that never tarnished, yet there was a commanding presence I wasn't sure how to respond to. She never talked about her love life. I had no idea if she had a steady boyfriend or if she went through guys like most people changed underwear. There was never that sparkle in her eye or the bounce in her step that said she'd been thoroughly fucked. I've never seen a woman who'd just had her brains fucked out not possess that light, that sparkle, about them. Like they're walking on cloud nine. It's a special look, and when you see it on enough women, you begin to recognize it. Josephine held her emotions close to the vest. I often wondered if she was still a virgin, even at twenty-seven.

Connor had shared a little bit of information with me when I discreetly asked. At least, I hope I'd been discreet. He never acted as though he thought my reasons for asking were anything beyond the general curiosity of learning about a new co-worker. God forbid he should realize that my feelings were slightly more engaged than a platonic friendship for his favorite girl. And we all knew the Josephine Bishop held a special place in Connor's heart. Even being his second-in-command, and best friend, he'd never told me why Josie was so special to him. He treated her like a younger sister. He was over-protective to a degree that was unusual.

I knew Connor had worked for Josie's father a couple years before she started working for Blacklight Securities.

But, I also knew that something happened to Josie before Connor came into the picture. That's what I couldn't figure out. Neither discussed it, but it further cemented their relationship to the point where Josie worshipped the ground Connor walked on, and Connor treated Josie as though she was as fragile as glass and would break with the slightest breeze.

I knew she wouldn't break though. She was much stronger than anyone knew, like tempered steel. But I wouldn't taint her with the darkness that surrounded me. I knew the minute she tried to get close that I would snuff out her light with the blackness that surrounded me. So, I avoided her. It was easier for everyone that way. Especially me. I'd had no idea the agony I would feel knowing she was now forever out of my reach. It was just another strike against me. Eventually, I'd break and destroy everything good in my life. Especially her.

"Miles."

My eyes closed at the softly spoken word at my back. I braced myself before slowly turning around to confront its owner. At only 5' 9", being tall was not a trait I'd been blessed with, and Josie was only a couple inches shorter than me, so we were almost eye-to-eye. Her trademark royal blue glasses sat perched on her pert little nose. Her short, blonde bob was tucked behind her ears, her bangs flopping in her face. Even though I knew she was twenty-seven, she continued to look exactly like that fresh-faced girl on her first day here.

Her youthful appearance only further emphasized the vast difference in our ages. My hair had turned to gray at my temples, and the wrinkles across my forehead and around my eyes and mouth only served to highlight the fact I was pushing middle-aged. At forty-two, I'd lived a rough life and it showed. Killing Malcolm had aged me even more.

Knowing I couldn't just stand there staring, I forced myself to acknowledge her. "What can I do for you, Josephine?"

She always wrinkled her nose when I called her Josephine. Calling her Josie was too personal, especially when I was trying to keep my distance from her. I refused to admit that I liked being the only one that called her Josephine.

"I need the reports on the Bullman case. I've run all the numbers through my computer and can't seem to find the discrepancy in the bank account. I know it's there though. Five million dollars doesn't disappear overnight. Something happened to it, I just need to find out what."

"You'll have to talk to Bryce. He's the one assigned to the case."

"Wait, Connor told me you were the one working it. When did Bryce take over?"

"A few days ago."

Her shoulders deflated as though someone had let all the air out of them. "Oh. I thought we'd be working together on this case."

I'd asked Connor if I could be reassigned to a different case when he'd told me that Josie was the analyst working on this one. He wasn't happy with my request and only reluctantly acquiesced when I pushed the issue. There were no questions asked, even though I knew he wanted to ask them.

"No, I'm working on the Grafton assignment."

"Okay. Well, if you need anything, please don't hesitate to ask me. I'm happy to help."

I gave an abrupt nod of thanks and left her standing there. I could feel her eyes boring through my back as I walked away. There was never a time when I couldn't feel her stare following me. At no time over the last six years had I not been fully aware of Josephine Bishop.

Get your copy of Redemption today!
http://amzn.to/2s7scmZ

Doms of Club Eden

Submission

Desire

Redemption

Protect

Betrayal

My Christmas Dom

Absolution

Love Undercover Series

In Too Deep

Striking Distance

Atonement (Coming 2020)

Other Books

Love Notes: A Dark Romance

SEALs in Love

Say Yes

Black Light: Possession

Saving Evie: A Brotherhood Protectors

ABOUT THE AUTHOR

LK Shaw is a traveling physical therapist assistant by day and author by night. When she isn't traveling for work, she resides in South Carolina with her high maintenance beagle mix dog, Miss P. An avid reader since childhood, she became hooked on historical romance novels in high school. She now reads, and loves, all romance sub-genres, with dark romance and romantic suspense being her favorite. LK enjoys traveling and chocolate. Her books feature hot alpha heroes and the strong women they love.

Want a FREE short story? Be sure to sign up for my newsletter and download your copy of A Birthday Spanking, a Doms of Club Eden prequel!
http://bit.ly/LKShawNewsletter

LK loves to interact with readers. You can follow her on any of her social media:

LK Shaw's Club Eden: https://www.facebook.com/
groups/LKShawsClubEden
Author Page: www.facebook.com/LKShawAuthor
Author Profile: www.facebook.com/AuthorLKShaw
IG: @LKShaw_Author
Amazon: www.amazon.com/author/lkshaw
Bookbub: https://www.bookbub.com/authors/lk-shaw
Website: www.lkshawauthor.com

Made in the USA
Columbia, SC
11 April 2020